Donna D. Wade

Wisteria Trees and Honeybees

A Winding Journey—
Heritage to Home

Donna D. Wade

PUBLISH AMERICA

PublishAmerica
Baltimore

Happy Birthday, Pat!

Love,
Loris & Jimmie Powers

Hardcover 978-1-4489-3471-3
Softcover 978-1-4489-8986-7
PUBLISHED BY PUBLISHAMERICA, LLLP
www.publishamerica.com
Baltimore

Printed in the United States of America

In memory of
my mother

"Gone but not forgotten"

Acknowledgments

To my husband Scott...
who always encouraged me to follow my dreams, even when the
path sometimes seemed to take us uphill.

To my children, Brandon Scott and Chris Danielle...
who have always been and continue to be my inspiration.

To Mr. and Mrs. Eugene Ipock...
who gave of themselves unselfishly and showed me the meaning
of being a Christian.

To Anne Sampson...
who always thought of me as her child, even when I wasn't, and
loved me like I was perfect, even when I wasn't. I am most
certain that it will hurt when I fall off of the pedestal that she has
put me on.

Preface

Wisteria is a vigorous, twining vine used widely in landscaping. Among its attributes are hardiness, vigor, longevity and the ability to climb high. Wisteria is valued for the beautiful, large clusters of flowers that spring forth beginning in mid-spring and continuing on through the summer months. The blossom clusters, cascading much like grapes, come in a variety of colors and emit the most wonderful of fragrances.

With its almost mesmerizing fragrance and beautiful blossoms, Wisteria is at the top of my list of favorite things. On the other hand, if wisteria is left unattended, it can quickly grow out of control, eventually harming its surroundings in the process.

Life is very much the same.

Wisteria Trees and Honeybees is a journey of self-discovery, faith and survival. Maggie and her siblings are torn apart at an early age but once she becomes an adult, she makes it her goal to reunite and heal her family. Many times along the way, success seems just beyond her reach and sometimes life seems out of control.

One generation of secrets seems destined to keep her family apart but ultimately, it is secrets that bring them together.

Introduction

Maggie's first inclination had been to boycott the funeral but after thinking long and hard, had finally given in to her sense of duty and decided to attend. She was almost forty years old and yet she still found funerals to be not simply uncomfortable but almost unbearable. The mere thought of a funeral brought back to mind a time some thirty years ago; the images still as fresh as though it were only yesterday. The coffin, with its pale pink satin lining, precariously perched on the velvet-skirted stand; her mother, in a powder blue gown with the two creases showing its brand-newness; her swollen hands folded neatly upon her abdomen. The people passing by were saying she looked "at peace." To Maggie, she just looked gone.

Yes, Maggie tried to avoid funerals. In fact, she had decided to be late for her own, if at all possible. Sure, she had made the decision to come but now that she was here, she wasn't quite sure why. After all, she and her grandmother had never really had much of a relationship. Early on, it had been a bad relationship and in later years, no relationship at all. Nonetheless, here she was, having taken the afternoon off from work, without pay no less, to attend. Was it out of a sense of responsibility? She had almost always been one to do the right thing, even when she would have preferred not to. Was that why she was here now or was it merely to verify the obvious?

On second thought, yes, she was sure.

It was a dreary, miserable afternoon. The temperature was hot, up seven degrees from yesterday, and with the precipitation that kept coming and going, the humidity was almost overbearing. The sunshine had been nice and bright before lunch. Early afternoon brought two hours of the sun playing peek-a-boo with the clouds and now, at three o'clock, the weather had done a complete about-face, a one-eighty. But then, that's what one could expect from the weather in South Carolina. Too, the weather was entirely appropriate, considering the circumstances. It seemed to Maggie that, more times than not, funeral services were held in less than optimum weather conditions.

Maggie, only halfway paying attention, sat next to her younger sister, Bethany. As the pre-prescribed ritual played out before her, her mind was busy with its own business, quietly noticing, with great interest, a couple of things. This funeral, unlike that of her mother's, was held at the funeral home, in a special room. In this "parlor" as they called it, one would have expected to see a large group gathered to pay their last respects to an individual who had made an indelible impression on their lives. In contrast to the expected, here today to offer condolences and consolation to loved ones left behind, were less than a dozen people; make that a baker's dozen, if you include the three staff members. Maggie also noticed, as she circled the room with her peripheral vision, that there was only one flower; one flower and no tears.

Now some might argue that to cry at a funeral or memorial service is inappropriate behavior and certainly, in some cultures, a lack of emotional display may be quite proper. Here, in the southern state of South Carolina, emotional outbursts are not only an ordinary part of life, whether at a birth, death or any event in between, but are expected to a certain degree. Still, it seemed more than a little odd to Maggie that there were only thirteen, mostly dry-eyed, people.

Certainly, it was no surprise that Maggie and Bethany did not cry. Bethany was there simply to lend a shoulder to Aunt Louise who had been Grandma's caretaker, chief cook and bottle washer if you will, for the past few years. That had been made even more complicated by Grandma's dementia which had progressed so far as to make her totally incapacitated.

After a few words by the preacher in the viewing room, the service continued with the ceremonial parade through town to the designated "resting" place. The site that had been chosen for Grandma's interment was near the back of Rosemont Memorial Cemetery, one of the oldest cemeteries in Richland County. Grandma had most likely chosen it when she buried her son, Gerald, just a few years earlier.

The graveside service was short and as unemotional as the first part had been, making Maggie wonder why they even bothered to have a graveside service. As everyone filed past the simple wooden coffin, the rain, which had diminished to barely a mist, slowly began its accent to a steady stream. The last notes of "Amazing Grace" began to fade away and Maggie's mind drifted back to a time, long, long ago. To the beginning...

PART I

THE BEGINNING

Chapter 1
Home Sweet Home

The eight hundred square foot house was situated squarely on a two acre lot on a long, lonely, almost desolate, stretch of road halfway between town and nowhere. Maggie's father had moved to this rural area of Calhoun County from Charleston in the early 1950s. After he and Momma got married, he had built the house for her. As a simple shotgun house, you could stand in the front door and see right through the house and out the back door. Still, it was adequate enough with its three bedrooms, kitchen and living room. The wood stove sat obtrusively in the middle of the house; it's strategic location offering warmth to all who entered. The faded and worn vinyl linoleum floor dared not try to hide all the years of use. The walls, once painted a clean white, were now dingy with age and smoke. The coolness of the faded, unimposing exterior fell far short of disclosing all of the color and excitement that was the norm on the inside.

The screened-in back porch ran the entire width of the house, offering shade on sunny days as well as shelter from the summer rains. In the colder months, it provided a covered area in which to hang the family's laundry. The porch was concrete and was not only a home for the wringer washing machine but was also home to the big, round aluminum tub that the family used for its weekly baths. Perhaps the most valuable purpose the porch served was that of protecting the hand-pumped water spigot and sink.

Maggie's family might have been considered well-off before her daddy died, as they did not have to go across the yard to fetch water; rather, they just had to go out onto the back porch. They did, however, still have the need to go outside to the outhouse but their outhouse was considered superior to many in the surrounding area. Like most outhouses of the time, it had the typical half-moon shape cut into the door to allow light in and odors out. What made this outhouse special was the fact that it had two seats and even had space in between for the Sears and Roebuck catalog. The Sears and Roebuck catalog served a dual purpose. First off, it served as a reading and shopping source. In fact, many of the family's clothing and household items were obtained through mail order or ordered by phone and then picked up at the catalog store in town. Secondly, and perhaps more importantly, the outdated catalogs were used as toilet paper. Literally. Money was scarce and could not be wasted on paper made and sold just to be thrown away.

However, that was ages ago and things had changed so much.

The cemetery was just about a half mile from the house and Maggie often went there with her momma. Though the marble headstone was cut into a basic rectangle and engraved simply, it seemed to give so much comfort to Momma, especially during the hard times following that cold day six months earlier when her daddy had died. He had been buried just outside the garden wall of the Siever Family Cemetery, next to baby Edward who had died just five years earlier. Momma knelt on the ground, resting her head on the cold headstone, waiting patiently for the peace that so often seemed to elude her. During this quiet time, Maggie busied herself, wandering around the cemetery, picking up leaves and reading names on headstones; some of them dating back over a hundred years. Sometimes it seemed as if Momma would have stayed there all day long if not for the eight-month-old fetus waiting inside her, clamoring to get out.

Maggie, being the third step in the staircase that was her family, had the good fortune of being able to benefit from the knowledge of her two older siblings, Shelby and Henry. At the same time, she also had the responsibility of helping to care for her younger sister, Bethany. This gave her a maturity and sensitivity that most children of her age did not possess. Though Maggie was quiet and reserved, this was just what Momma needed when visiting the cemetery. Sometimes, they just sat together in silence, each one breathing in the strength that was their father and husband. When serenity had once again returned to their innermost places, Maggie and her momma returned home to the never-ending carnival of events. That was to be expected in a four-child, six-room house in the rural South.

Once, there had been a gas station sitting up the hill by the road, right in front of the house. It had been built by Maggie's daddy soon after he built the house. That was not very long after he and Momma got married. Momma had never shied away from a challenge and had always been a hard worker. She had helped Daddy run the store, day after day; she mostly worked inside while he took care of the gas pumps and the other outside stuff. She took time off only long enough to give birth to their children. That meant she got a break from the gas station as they added one to their litter every year or so of their marriage.

There were very many farms in the area but few service stations. This made Momma and Daddy's business a good one with a large customer base. As families and tobacco allotments grew, so did their business. Though they did not offer anything extravagant in their store, only the basic necessities, they ran a successful and thriving business. Successful, that is, until the day the store burned down. No one had ever said for sure exactly what had happened but there had been lots of speculation. One of the rumors was that in addition to running the store, Daddy had used it as a front for a moonshine business. The story was that Daddy had made a deal with one of his long-time customers but when he began hearing that the law was beginning to really crack down on moonshiners, Daddy backed out. The customer, having disgruntled customers of his own, apparently decided to seek satisfaction through revenge so he burglarized the store, taking whatever he thought he could sell and then set the whole place on fire.

Now, with the store gone and Daddy gone, it had become harder and harder for Momma to provide the things that her family needed. She already sewed most of their clothes, many from washed flour and chicken feed sacks.

Each spring, Momma would ask the neighbor, George, to bring his mule to the house. After George had plowed and tilled the half acre spot of land next to the cinderblock garage, Momma and Grandma would begin the time-consuming chore of planting a vegetable garden. Though they were in charge, all of the children assisted as well, not with just the planting, but also with the harvesting, shelling, shucking and canning. It was a wonderful garden with everything from string beans and corn to speckled butter beans, cucumbers, okra, peas, squash, tomatoes and watermelons. Of course, it had to be a wonderful, extensive garden; the family depended on it. All except for the okra, that is. Even when the okra was fried, the slimy centers made these the least favorite of all the things the garden offered, at least to the children. Momma and Grandma, on the other hand, absolutely loved them. Nonetheless, the majority of their food supply would come from this ever-so-important lifeline. After all of the needed vegetables were planted, Momma found a bit of space at the edge to plant a few hills of flowers. She always tried to look for the blessings in life and the flowers reminded her that, even when hard times came, life could still be beautiful.

Momma did not talk too much about favorite things because she was very meek and modest. She was not at all materialistic and most definitely not a vain person. She did not need or want a lot. She was humble in that regard and actually had no true luxuries. Of course, even without her saying so, everybody knew that she loved the outdoors because every chance she got, she would sit outside, underneath the giant wisteria tree and watch the honeybees. As she laid her head back, the sweet smell of the wisteria would fill her nostrils and soothe her frazzled nerves. She would close her eyes and listen to nothing but the soft hum of the honeybees; occasionally even losing all track of time. The simple miracle of the wisteria flowers, how all the little petals, each beautiful in its own right, came together to form a larger, even more fantastic creation, was a wonder. The honeybees buzzed around the flowers, seeming to lack the need to ever stop and rest. They were an inspiration to her because, like herself, they had a hard life—work, work, work—but in the end, it was always sweet. Though the wisteria was Momma's favorite, she had an ever-expanding assemblage of orange tiger lilies too. Together, these made our house truly heavenly for Momma on those rare spring and summer days when she was granted a respite.

Chapter 2
Grandma

As summer got closer, and hotter, the time drew near for the baby to be born and so it was arranged for Grandma to move in. She had, of course, lived with them from time to time in a small apartment that Daddy had set up in the upper part of the garage situated right next to the house but she had never lived right there in the house with them. All that changed after Daddy died and Grandma moved into the house permanently with the rest of the family.

Grandma had made it clear right from the start that it was not by choice that she moved in; it was simply a necessity. Where would she have gone if not here? Sure, she had spent time at Aunt Louise's house as well as her own sister Maxine's. Each and every time though, something would happen—a falling out over this or that—and she'd wind up out again. Truth is, she had never really lived on her own, in her own house. She had never even had what you might call a regular job or a real job. She had always depended on someone else to help support her. Sure, she occasionally helped put in a barn of tobacco or pick a little cotton here and there, but a regular job, no. Moreover, as much as it seemed that her moving in would benefit Momma and the children, the reality was that Grandma was not one to be concerned for the well-being of others, even her own pregnant daughter.

Everyone who knew her could attest to the fact that Grandma had never been a very loving person. That character flaw was especially apparent to her very own grandchildren. Indeed, her dislike became more and more obvious once she was living in the house all the time. At least before, when Grandma was living in the garage apartment, Maggie and her brother and sisters could avoid her more easily. For the most part, they simply tried to stay out of Grandma's reach for, at the slightest provocation, she would switch them. What was worse, she would even send them out in the yard to pick the very switch she used to beat them. Anyone who knows anything about switches can tell you that a fresh switch is much more limber than an old, dried out one and can do much more damage. Then too, a long one is much more effective than a shorter one. Like a jelly fish, it was capable of wrapping around legs, arms and bodies, stinging as it struck. Of course, if a switch was returned with all the little knots scratched off, extra punishment was doled out. Sometimes Grandma would not even wait for a switch or fly swatter; she would just pick up whatever was around; a book, a spoon, a broom or a log.

It was not long after Sarah was born in July that it became quite evident that Momma would no longer be able to stay at home and raise her family as she had done before. She would have to find work away from home. She had become quite good as a tailor and very quickly found a job working in a sewing factory earning thirty dollars each week. With Momma away from home more than before and Grandma being responsible for the children on a daily basis, it became easier for her to take out her frustration on them. One day, Henry, who was about twelve at the time, began construction of a car, much like a downhill racer; no engine, only gravity and man power. He had "borrowed" two wheels from the lawn mower to use on the front of his car and his bicycle wheels on the back. Even though he would return the wheels to the lawn mower eventually, the simple fact that he had removed them in the first place aggravated Grandma tremendously. The longer he continued to ignore Grandma's ranting and raving, the more furious she became. In fact, she wasn't just mad, she was livid. She took off after Henry with a none-too-small tree limb in hand. When she realized that she was not going to be able to catch him, she threw the limb with all her might, all the while yelling, "Come back here, you hussy." That was her word alright. Hussy. Surprisingly, she did not normally use actual curse words but when you heard that word—hussy—you knew you were in big trouble. The limb whizzed by, missing Henry's head by just inches, landing with a thud in the weeds. With the sound of the thud came the realization that Henry was in more trouble than if he had been hit with the log. It was certainly a long evening for Henry as he waited in the woods next to the creek for Momma to get home from work.

The meager paycheck that Momma brought home each week made it next to impossible for her to take care of her growing family. Even having a garden and sewing the kids' clothes, what clothes she could, did not keep their heads above water throughout the whole month. It did not take too long for Momma to realize she needed even more help. While she was a proud woman, when it came to her children, she was not too proud to ask for help. From anyone. Now, once a month, Momma received coupons in the mail from the county

Social Service Department. The coupons allowed them to go down to the welfare office and pick up a few grocery items. Usually they selected cans of dried eggs and a big box of cheese. These items could be stretched and made to last. When they started home, they would stop by the bakery thrift store and pick up several loaves of out-of-date sandwich bread. It wasn't really stale; it was just past the date printed on the package and had to be removed from the regular grocery store shelves. It would last a long time, especially in the freezer. Everyone was always glad to get this small contribution and greatly appreciated it. Even so, after a while, cheese sandwiches and dried eggs grew a bit tiresome.

Even though Grandma had a dismal and sometimes dour disposition, everyone, even those who had wound up on the wrong end of her temper or her switch, had to admit she was an excellent seamstress. That is probably where Momma learned to sew so well. Along with all the other girls in her family, Grandma had taken up sewing as a young girl and had been sewing ever since. One of her specialties was kitchen aprons. She made aprons with bibs and aprons without bibs. Some even had ruffles on them and of course, all of them had pockets. After she had sewed up a good number, usually two to three dozen, in assorted patterns and colors, she would fold them just so and put them in a cardboard box she had picked up at the dime store. First, they would sell aprons to the neighbors. This sometimes worked out well for practically all of the women in the surrounding community were homemakers, and aprons were an absolute necessity in the kitchen, particularly on a farm. Here the women spent a good deal of time in the kitchen either cooking for large families or canning food for later.

If there were many aprons left, the family would make a trip the next weekend into St. Matthews, about fifteen or so miles to the west. Grandma had never learned to drive so that meant Momma had to drive her into town, even though she had already worked over a forty-five hour work week. Sales were sometimes better in town because the more well-off people lived in town and many had hired help who were required to wear aprons as part of their uniform. Even when they did not need new aprons, the city people sometimes bought one or two just to help out the family if they were feeling charitable. Maggie knew it and Shelby probably knew it too. Grandma never did the actual selling herself though. She usually required the oldest kids, Shelby and Henry, to peddle the homemade goods. It seemed a lot like begging and Maggie was sure they didn't like doing it. Sometimes they got a bit high headed and felt they were above this but Momma wasn't too proud and she quickly set them straight. She made them understand that sometimes "you just gotta do what you gotta do." After all, the few dollars made from the sale of aprons was enough to carry them through to the next month when the welfare coupons would arrive again.

After each sewing session, whether it was making quilts, aprons, or clothes, Grandma and Momma would gather all the material scraps and put them into a bag. Eventually, there would be enough scraps for Grandma to begin piecing together a new quilt. Finished quilts that were not needed at home would be added to the stack of aprons for selling on the next trip to town.

The actual making of a quilt was a time-consuming, multi-step process. First, Grandma would cut the small scraps into specific shapes and then sew them together into a pattern. The log cabin design was one of her favorite patterns, next to the Texas Star. The quilt top was then placed on top of a layer of cotton seed quilt batting and the quilt back which was typically a single color. Grandma used a big frame that looked like four tobacco sticks held together with nails. After being assembled, the frame was propped up on the backs of four strategically placed straight-back chairs. Since the actual stitching together of the quilt was all done by hand, this was a long-term project, usually taking several days; several days, that is, unless you had a quilting bee. A quilting bee involved having several ladies come over and spend an afternoon, or sometimes a whole day, quilting. It was considered a social event as much as anything and since Grandma was not really much of a socializer, most times she did the quilting herself, alone. That was fine with the younger children as this gave them a great play area and hideout under the quilt. As long as they did not mess up the quilt or frame, they were safe from Grandma's wrath.

Chapter 3
Snuff and Stuff

Grandma had always seemed old, at least to Maggie. Her bang-less, thinning hair was about a yard long but was always twisted tightly into a rope and then wound round and round until it made a small neat ball on the back of her head. She looked like an old schoolmarm, maybe even the *first* schoolmarm. The ball was held in place by four u-shaped hairpins. She wore small oval glasses that slid down her nose, allowing her to look at you through her dark bushy eyebrows. She kept her mouth drawn up so tight that her chin formed a sharp point, making her chin whiskers seem even longer. She had a twitch in her lip that probably came from all those years of dipping snuff. Railroad Mills. That was her brand. Snuff is soft and powdery like cocoa but its taste can vary from brand to brand. Unlike the Honeybee brand that Momma had taken to dipping, Railroad Mills was somewhat bitter tasting; but then, that suited Grandma's personality perfectly.

Honeybee snuff smelled good and tasted sweet; so good in fact that not only Maggie, but all the children, often tried to sneak into Momma's pocketbook and pilfer just a smidgen or two. They felt oh so grown, walking around with a pinch of snuff between their cheek and gum. One time, though, Maggie was not so lucky and did not achieve her mission. She had recently developed a risen in the bend behind her right knee and over about a week's time, it had gotten really red, swollen and painful. On this day, a Thursday, Momma had managed to get off work a few minutes early. Once she arrived home, she was confronted with the sight and sounds of a child in need of relief. She promptly began to work on the leg and, for more than ten minutes, tried to relieve the pressure by squeezing and mashing until the puss began to erupt. Maggie, as a rule, had a pretty high tolerance for pain. In fact, just last year, her brother Henry had pulled her two front teeth with nothing more than a pair of pliers. But some body parts are more sensitive than others and some kinds of wounds just naturally cause more pain. After much suffering and a wash cloth full of tears, the risen was deflated and Maggie was resting semi-comfortably on the couch, a red couch that Momma had bought on credit at the Bargain Barn. Momma did not make it a habit of buying things on credit, especially things not edible; however, the old couch had finally worn through to the springs and had become a safety hazard. There was simply no resurrecting it.

After lying still for a good fifteen minutes more, Maggie began to feel better and was soon back to her old self. She looked around and, after making sure that Momma was still watching her favorite show, *The Arthur Smith Show*, Maggie jumped up from the couch, running toward Momma's bedroom. That is where Momma kept her snuff—in her pocketbook on a shelf, above the dresser, just out of reach. Just as Maggie was approaching the door to the bedroom, she lost her footing and fell, sliding head first into the wooden door jam. Not only did she not get the snuff, she acquired another wound, a grim reminder that crime does not pay. Funny how a saying that meant nothing yesterday can just all of a sudden make sense.

Years ago, the Leonards had raised pigs, but when the last one was sold after Daddy died, they simply could not afford to buy more piglets, much less the feed for them. So now, besides the food that was grown in the small garden at the edge of the property, the Leonards relied heavily on the chickens and guineas that they still had. In addition to having plenty of eggs to eat themselves, they were able to sell a few whenever they had extras. Sometimes, they even traded them for needed items down at Mr. Murphy's store. Plus, they were able to have a chicken to eat every Sunday or two. Even though the chickens and guineas were kept in a fenced area, they were forever trying to fly the coop so all the birds had to have their wings clipped on a regular basis. The guineas loved to sleep on top of the house and somehow managed to get up there night after night, clipped wings and all. The chickens spent their nights inside a small chicken coop. The coop was nothing more than planks nailed haphazardly together to form a twelve-by-twelve cubicle covered with a tin roof. Inside were several rows of "poles," attached horizontally, each one about a foot higher than the last. These provided places for the birds to roost.

After the outhouse burned to the ground, the chicken coop provided a private place, at least for the most part, to pee and poop, without running the risk of stepping in it later; that is, if you were careful getting down off the roosts so as not to fall. It was also the perfect place to smoke the cigarettes that Shelby and Henry managed to swipe from time to time.

Sometimes they could not sneak Momma's cigarettes so they had to come up with a Plan B. The group had learned to be quite resourceful and so there always seemed to be a Plan B. This time, it meant they would have to smoke "pretend" tobacco. The older kids became especially practiced at making pipes from corncobs and bamboo reeds. First a dried out corncob was cut to about one inch long and hollowed out to form a bowl. A hole was cut on the side to insert a small hollow bamboo reed. They then stuffed the pipe with dried grass or paper, most anything. The end of the reed was placed in the mouth, held between the teeth. What a fine looking pipe! They would sit back and smoke it just as if they were somebody. A pipe usually lasted through several smokings before needing to be replaced. Whoever said that necessity is the mother of invention sure knew what they were talking about.

Grandma's wardrobe was very sparse. It did not include normal undergarments such as bras or step-ins; rather, she chose to wear only slips and housedresses. Maggie and the others could not figure out the reason for this since Momma certainly did not dress this way and was always properly dressed. Instead of using the outhouse like everyone else, and the chicken coop or woods after the outhouse burned, Grandma would just go outside, right in the middle of the yard in the broad open daylight, to pee. There she'd stand, legs spread apart. In a minute or two she'd begin leaking. She never said a word, only stood there. When she was finished, she simply fanned herself with her dress until she was dry. If she passed gas during the episode, she'd say, "Whew wee!" just to let everyone else know that she knew she had done it. Even if you had not known she had passed gas, you sure knew it when she went to caterwauling, "Whew wee!" all over the place! If she had to do more than simply pee, she usually held it until after dark when she could use the old collard pot that sat in her bedroom, right there next to the bed.

Being curious like kids are, the children never missed an opportunity to try to discover what was under the housedress. They simply could not believe that Grandma did not wear any undergarments. Henry, being a boy, was naturally more adventurous and daring. His favorite trick was to lie on the floor, pretending to be asleep, peeping whenever Grandma walked by. If she ever figured out what he was doing, she never let on. Try as he might, Henry never did solve the mystery. There was always a great darkness underneath the material that surrounded Grandma's more than ample figure.

Chapter 4
Snug as a Bug in a Rug

When it came to sleeping arrangements for five children and two adults, it took some finessing to find a solution that worked; worked that is, for almost everyone. The front bedroom was really quite small and barely had room for one double bed and a single-wide roll-away bed. Henry slept on the rollaway bed, which was actually rather uncomfortable since the bar underneath tended to make itself known right through the quilted mattress. Being the oldest girls, Shelby and Maggie shared the remaining bed.

The middle bedroom was Momma's room. She shared her regular sized bed with her youngest daughter, Sarah. Sarah was very small so they had plenty of room to sleep contentedly in spite of the fact that Sarah always slept with one leg hoisted over Momma's side or either crossways the bed.

The back bedroom had been Momma and Daddy's room but after Daddy was gone, Momma simply could not sleep in there anymore so it became Grandma's bedroom. Grandma would have really rather had her own room and she certainly would have gotten no argument from anyone, but with so many children, it simply was not practical for her to sleep alone while the other beds already accommodated two people each.

When Grandma first moved in, Shelby had been the one assigned to sleep with her but as time passed, the spot was relinquished first to Maggie and most recently to Bethany. After Bethany was assigned, against her will, to sleep with Grandma, she quickly discovered why Maggie and Shelby had been so disturbed by the notion.

If Grandma was scary during the daytime, then nighttime increased the horror by at least double. First off, she did not sleep in a night gown or pajamas. In fact, she must not have even owned either one. She slept in her slip, a simple cotton slip; the same one she had worn all day. Secondly, she did not wear step-ins, bloomers, or any kind of undergarment. Not even a brazier. Not only that, but she could make some of the strangest noises when she slept, much like a wild animal that had been caged. And then of course, there were the regular outbursts of nauseating fumes. If you were unlucky enough to already be in the bed but not yet asleep, you had to fight the urge to laugh while, at the same time, keep the gag reflex at bay and protect yourself from the imminent danger of suffocation from noxious fumes. If the gases emanating from this bedroom could have been bottled and sold, there might never be an energy crisis.

As if all this wasn't enough, there was also the issue of "Bloody Bones and Stain Steel." Neither of these horrors was present until Grandma moved in so there was no question that she brought them with her and controlled them or at least, allowed them.

Grandma had always had strict rules for thunderstorms and bedtime. Actually, she was strict about everything but just more so about these two things. During thunderstorms, candles were lit and all electrical devices, lights and TV included, were turned off and unplugged. Everyone was required to sit quietly in the semi-dark until the storm passed. There was to be no talking, no playing, no nothing, except praying. Grandma said the thunderstorms were God's way of getting our attention and we'd better listen. Sometimes the family shutdown would last minutes, at other times, much longer.

Bedtime was similar in that, at lights out, Grandma demanded total quiet once the nightly prayer was said. If the children did not all lie still and go straight to sleep, Grandma could be heard throughout the house threatening to call Bloody Bones and Stain Steel. Bloody Bones lived in the hole in the ceiling that gave access to the tiny attic space above. He must have been the devil or some close relative of the devil. In any case, after Grandma and Bloody Bones moved in, no one ever went into the attic again. Whatever Christmas decorations or other stuff had been placed there, remained there, unclaimed.

The house had no central air conditioning, only the open windows. Of course, Grandma had the stainless steel fan which sat next to the passenger-side of her bed on a chair. The fan had a green metal motor and green metal blades. The blades, once covered by a protective shield on the front, now whizzed around completely exposed since the screws securing the cover had come unscrewed and had been lost long, long ago. Any stray fingers or other body parts were subject to removal or damage if care was not taken to remain clear. Sure, it was simply a fan by day, but by night, the shadow-making moonlight and the eerie screeching of its motor transformed it into "Stain Steel."

The other side of Grandma's bed was "guarded" by an open collard pot. At least it used to be a collard pot; now it was used by Grandma as a night pot. Much of the white porcelain enamel had long ago chipped away to the point of revealing the black metal underneath. The bits of enamel that remained were stained a most undesirable color.

Any child daring to slip out of the covers would be threatened by these things on a nightly basis. All these things, and do not forget—no "step-ins," made it a traumatic event to be Grandma's bed feller. Luckily for Bethany, the daily ritual of emptying the pot was delegated to Henry, being the only boy.

Often, Bethany would try to go to bed earlier than the others, trying to stake her claim to one of the other beds. One time, she had even taken a quilt and hid *behind* Momma's bed, which was situated catty-cornered in her room. Maggie hoped that the big space in the corner would make it harder for her to be spotted from the doorway. Try as she might, she was always returned to Grandma's room. It didn't take long to learn to sleep with the covers pulled up to her chin, arms tucked neatly inside, being careful not to roll over.

Once in a great while Bethany would be lucky and would manage to escape from Grandma's room. Maggie absolutely loved to have her back scratched so occasionally, Bethany could worm her way into Maggie and Shelby's bed by offering to give a free back scratch. Add alcohol rubs on top of that and she was sure to be in the "big girls club." Occasionally, on other lucky nights, she made her way into Momma's bed, even if it meant sleeping crossways at the foot.

Chapter 5
Fun, Fun, Fun

Toys, especially expensive or complicated ones, were scarce around the Leonard home. Other than the small things like jack rocks, marbles and sling shots, which the kids bought with their saved up tobacco money, toys were not bought except on birthdays and Christmas. Henry had received the shiny, red bike for Christmas the year before. Although it was technically Henry's bike, he never minded sharing with the other kids. That was just how Momma taught them, share and share alike. Of course, the smaller kids, Bethany and Sarah, were not big enough to ride it because it was, after all, a "big" boy's bike. Even Maggie wasn't quite big enough to ride completely solo. She had to climb on the bike by first standing on the front porch and then shoving off with one foot. She wasn't tall enough for her feet to reach the ground but, by using the porch as a step, she was able to get it going and slip her toes onto the peddles. Once Maggie was on that bike, except for the fact that she had to ride standing up, she was as big as anyone and boy, did she absolutely love it! She would fly around the front yard, zip around by the chicken coop and then cruise around to the back yard, remembering to duck under the clothes line. She reached the ground soon enough though, for invariably when she rounded the old outhouse, she'd lose control and slam into the woodpile. No matter how many times she fell though, she never lost her will to try just one more time. She was relentless.

After scrimping and saving for one whole year, Momma finally saved enough money and bought a merry-go-round from the Bargain Barn store. In a family this size, with an age spread of ten years, it was not just difficult but almost impossible to find something that could be enjoyed by everyone. But this time was different. This merry-go-round was indeed something that all the kids could use. Sure, it only had four seats, but still, with four riding and one pushing, it worked out perfectly.

Mostly, though, the kids were dependent on their own imaginations, and each other, for entertainment. Sometimes they played in the old, black broken-down Plymouth parked in the back yard. Its engine did not run but, other than the four flat tires, it *looked* great. Anyway, it wasn't used for anything except as a storage place for the big bags of food for Black Jack, the family German shepherd. Maggie, Bethany and Sarah particularly liked playing "family" in the car. They would take turns being the mommy, the daddy and the baby. Not very often, but occasionally, Henry would reluctantly agree to play. When he did, he naturally played the daddy, which allowed them to then have two babies. Twins ran in Momma's side of the family as far back as anyone could recollect, so it was natural for these two babies to be twins as well. They went shopping and to school, to church and fishing. Occasionally, they would even "drive" to

Lake Burleigh. On the way, they would munch on the "corn chips" they had dug out of the dog food bag.

The other place that they liked to "drive to" was "South of the Border." They had only been there once or twice in real life, but it had made a lasting impression. Situated just south of the North Carolina line on Interstate 95, "South of the Border" was only about a ninety minute drive. Of course, you never had to ask "how much farther" since there were "South of the Border" signs almost every five miles letting you know how close you were getting. At least it seemed that way. You knew you had finally arrived when you spotted the two hundred foot sombrero tower and then the hundred foot Pedro. There was an amusement park and lots of shopping and food. Best of all, you could buy fireworks. Of course, due to financial restraints and safety issues, they mostly just bought sparklers and ate hotdogs between Pedro's legs. The overall appearance of the place might have been gaudy to the tenth degree but the colors and smells were awe-inspiring to the children who had never really ventured very far from home. And so, while children could be fascinated time and time again by the sight, most adults probably would have had their fill after one stop at the inter-state paradise.

Other times they would climb up on top of the old Plymouth and then climb up on top of the horse stable. After tying a towel around each of their necks, they'd jump off, one by one, each one declaring to be the greatest super hero. Sometimes they just jumped back onto the hood of the car; other times, when they were feeling especially daring, Shelby, Henry and Maggie would jump all the way down to the ground. Shelby and Henry never suffered any broken bones, only an occasional sprained ankle or wrist but Maggie did have one nasty spill that resulted in a broken collar bone. That ended her super hero days.

Henry was brilliant and definitely all boy; he was immensely imaginative and resourceful. He loved to tinker on things and was constantly trying to figure out how and why they worked. He especially liked things with motors. On a regular basis, he would dismantle the lawn mower and sometimes he was even able to get it back together by himself. Other times he was not so lucky. One Christmas, Santa brought Maggie a teeny, tiny record player that played plastic three-inch records. It was possibly the best thing Santa had ever brought her, at least up to that point. Needless to say, Maggie just loved it. Henry loved it too but for a different reason. He was very curious to see how it worked— how those little plastic records could make such a beautiful sound. So, just two days after Christmas, he took the whole thing apart. Only problem was, when he finally got it back together, it did not work, ever again.

Maggie's daddy had always loved animals and he had owned a parrot named Pete. Pete must have belonged to a pirate at one time or at the very least a boatman of some sort, for he certainly had the vocabulary of a sailor. Daddy had also owned a chimpanzee named Dolly. Both animals could be a bit cantankerous and in fact tended to bite strangers with little or no provocation. Dolly was particularly jealous of women, especially when Daddy was around. As time went on, Dolly became more and more aggressive until the day she attacked Aunt Louise. That was the day she found herself on the wrong end of a shotgun.

Dolly had lived in a giant cage very similar to the cages where circus animals were kept. The cage was about eight feet long, three feet high, four feet wide and was on wheels so it could easily be moved around from one place to another. With Dolly gone, Henry decided that the cage would be perfect for some new adventures. With the help of the others, Henry cleaned out the cage and away they went. When the kids tired of it being a circus wagon, they simply changed their minds and the cage became something else. One day it would be a taxi, the next day it would be a school bus.

Shelby, Henry, Maggie, Bethany and Sarah each took their turns being the engine, the animals and the passengers.

Summertime brought adventures of a different sort. All the kids loved to play in water and the bar pit made a wonderful swimming hole. In truth, the bar pit was just a ditch between the road and where the store used to be. After the store burned down, part of its counter top, though melted and charred, was found in the ditch. That's how it became known as the bar pit. The bar pit was about three feet deep in some places and not so deep in other places. That made it easy for the older kids—Shelby and Henry—to swim and for the younger ones—Maggie, Bethany and Sarah—to "pretend" swim by crawling around on their hands and knees. Henry even made a bridge by dragging a two by eight plank from the dilapidated horse barn and placing it across the ditch. Cottonmouth snakes had been seen from time to time in the barn and around the water so Shelby and Henry made a point to watch out for them.

Peter's Pond was just about a half mile down Black Swamp Road and then a quarter mile down a narrow path though the thick woods. Being over three acres, the pond gave plenty of room to fish, swim or simply splash around in the water. The water was much clearer than the other ponds in the area because it had a sandy bottom instead of the usual black silt and dirt. This made spotting fish a cinch. While Grandma did not swim or even get in the water, she would sit on the fringe around the pond and fish. Her fishing pole was nothing more than a long, stiff cane pole rigged with fishing line, an orange bobber and a hook. There was no reel, but then she did not need one. She was a very attentive fisherperson and the instant a fish dared to nibble on the freshly dug earthworm firmly attached to the hook, Grandma whipped the pole up and out of the water so fast the fish went sailing through the air, up and over her head. Bethany or Maggie was usually right there, waiting to remove the poor, traumatized fish from the well-laid trap. As Grandma fished, the other kids played quietly by the water, careful not to disturb the fishing ambience. As soon as Grandma got tired of fishing, though, the fun began with everyone, everyone except Grandma that is, jumping happily in the water, all cares washed away, at least for the time being.

Before the fire, there had been two big, round Coca Cola signs mounted on a post outside Daddy's store. Luckily, because they were metal, the heat did not damage them very badly. One day Henry got the idea that the two signs could be used as a boat. He considered the idea for a moment. They looked just deep enough that they might float and, if he joined the two together somehow, they would be pretty stable and might even be capable of carrying several people. So he did just that—joined the two signs securely together by attaching wire through the mounting holes. Then, with the signs turned face down, he laid a one by six plank on top, extending over both ends of the signs. This boat, being wide and steady made for a very stable ride and created a round-trip ticket for many wonderful excursions, both in the summertime and wintertime.

When the weather was warm, the Coke sign boat became a seaworthy vessel capable of carrying all five children up and down the ditch, I mean "river." Of course, this boat was not quite as exciting as Henry's previous attempt at boat making. That had been literally a roof tin boat. He had removed a sheet of the tin roof from the old horse barn and then proceeded to carefully shape it into a canoe shape. Then he filled the nail holes with tar as best he could. Once the boat was delivered safely to the bar pit, the only decision left was who would be the lucky one to test it out. Now everyone loved and looked up to Henry so it was not a matter of who would volunteer; rather the question was whom would Henry choose. As it turned out, Maggie was the chosen one. Henry had undoubtedly figured that while she was fairly small she was still old enough to handle the test. Maggie sat in the dead center of the boat just as she had been instructed and Henry gently pushed the boat away from the shoreline. Just as the boat reached the center of the waterway, it sank, right to the bottom. The good news was that "right to the bottom" only meant three feet and, while that was deeper than Maggie would have liked since she could not yet really swim, it was not so much life-threatening as it was just plain scary. Perhaps Henry had known more than he had let on.

In the wintertime, the Coke signs became something else. Once separated, the signs became dueling sleds, racing across the frozen water of the "bar pit." Being round and smooth on the bottom, they glided gracefully over the ice and snow-covered ground too. It was especially fun as they bounced wildly over the snow-banked tree stumps and limbs in the field between their house and the Marvins' house on the adjacent property. What a strange sight it must have been for strangers driving by to see them playing in the snow with their sock-covered hands and bread bag-covered feet.

Maggie's family owned a nineteen inch black and white television which was connected to an antenna mounted on a pole outside next to the house. Every single time they changed the channel, someone would have to go outside and turn the antenna pole until the picture came in clear. This was a small inconvenience, considering the enjoyment they got from their favorite shows. The Grand Ole Opry, Mutual of Omaha's Wild Kingdom, The Ed Sullivan Show; boy, did they love these shows. Saturday night, the favorite TV watching night, was spent watching "Will C's Red Eye Cinema," hosted by Will C. Morgan. He played his favorite scary movies for those brave enough to stay up late to watch them. The movies shown definitely separated the men from the boys, so to speak. Clearly, Bethany and Sarah were too young to be able to withstand the horror that was sure to come to those night owls. In fact, they would probably have nightmares for weeks but Maggie, Henry and Shelby all loved to torture themselves with the frightening shows. It was standard operating procedure for the last one to leave the room to turn off the television and close the curtains in the family room before going to bed. Problem was that, on many of these Saturday night events, the last one would be Maggie, the youngest of the three. Usually, she was too scared to get near the television, much less the exposed windows. After all, you could never be quite sure of what might be lurking in the darkness. Shelby and Henry knew this. Just the same, week after week, they tortured Maggie for a few minutes before coming to the rescue.

The woods that surrounded the Leonard family house contained many old hardwood trees. They were tall and thick and made excellent choices for tree houses and that is just what many of them became. Henry was a natural born construction engineer and knew just how to go about building the perfect tree house. Under his direction, the crew built four tree houses around the family's property. First they would construct a simple platform between three or four trees, making it as high up in the air as possible. This gave them a perfect vantage point from which to watch birds and other animals such as turtles, foxes and rabbits. It also gave the lookout an advantage over anyone sneaking up on them. The natural canopy of the surrounding trees helped to create a protective covering over and around the tree house, camouflaging them and giving a small amount of protection from the elements. Though they sometimes tried to make the tree houses different, the design for each one usually turned out basically the same. Fallen tree limbs were laid horizontally across the standing tree branches with decking made from leftover boards and cut limbs covered with cardboard. There was one way in and one way out. Access to the clubhouses was by makeshift ladders constructed by nailing odd bits of lumber or discarded tobacco sticks horizontally to the tree trunk. The only acceptable exit was by sliding down a rope attached to an upper limb and going down through a hole in the platform.

Before being allowed in the clubhouse, a secret password was always required. That was sometimes hard since the password was subject to change randomly, whenever Henry decided. More than once, Maggie had not been allowed to join the others in the club because she could not come up with the newly revised password. Henry had most likely changed the password just as she was approaching just to aggravate her. He had certainly done it many times before.

One time, after being turned away, Maggie and Bethany, who were only about eleven months apart in age, decided they would go off and make their own clubhouse. They worked for hours chopping down small pines with their daddy's old hatchet that they had found in the garage. When they thought they had enough timbers, they began to stack them, being extra careful to interlock the corners. Eventually, the walls were about shoulder high. Only then did they realize that Maggie had been stacking from the outside of the structure and Bethany had been stacking from the inside. When all was said and done, they had actually "fenced" Bethany in. There had been no plan for a door. Apparently, there had not been much of a plan at all, really, except to build *something*. They quickly learned that even with teamwork, the best results would come with better planning.

Often times, the Leonard children spent so much time in the woods, they came home at the end of the day with more than just a few good stories to share. Sometimes, they came home covered with redbugs, or chiggers. These parasites were all but microscopic, their tiny, red selves visible only through extremely careful inspection. They might have been small but the effect they had on the human body was anything but small. The areas they preferred, mostly under the armpits, under a waistband or in the protected area around the genitals, suffered from the nagging itching that the bugs caused. On the occasions that the kids' outings resulted in redbug infestation, they were treated to a gasoline bath. Yep, Momma would be forced to wash them down thoroughly with a washcloth dipped in a basin of gasoline. If there were only a few redbug spots, they might be lucky enough to get by with a dab of fingernail polish. Of course, if that did not smother the pests, the gasoline was brought out.

While Momma did not like to sing in public, there was no question that she loved and appreciated music. She still had the old upright piano with its five-foot high back that Daddy had bought for her. Though she wanted to be able to play, she never really learned. Instead, once in a while she would just sit and tinker on the keys. Still, when she was happy, she whistled or hummed. When she was sad, she still hummed, just a different sort of tune. This trait was passed down to her children for many of them loved to sing, or at least loved to pretend to sing. Bethany had even entered and won the Clancey School talent contest by singing *Me and My Shadow*. Not bad for a second grader. At home, Maggie, Bethany, and Sarah especially, loved to sit in the grass on the hill and sing the Pebbles and Bamm Bamm song *Let the Sun Shine In*. The more they practiced, the better they became. Henry, who at first couldn't carry a tune in a bucket, soon joined the group and became one of its best singers. And of course, he did a right fair Bamm Bamm impression too.

The old merry-go round, with its four seats, was still fun too, especially when Henry propped two of the four legs up on cinderblocks. This made a great tilt-o-whirl and even added enough excitement that the older kids wanted to ride too. Yep, they were always willing to try something new; safe or unsafe. It was okay. After all, Momma and Grandma were inside watching "The Porter Wagoner Show."

Summertime brought occasional trips to Lake Burleigh. Back in the sixties, only one side of the lake had been developed. There were a few cottages scattered here and there but the main lakeside attractions were the arcade and amusement park. The arcade housed lots and lots of games to throw your money away on but, since money was a most prized commodity, time was better spent at the amusement park where you were guaranteed something for your dime. Momma and Aunt Louise kept a close eye on Sarah, Bethany, and Maggie as they climbed aboard the carousel. As the horses circled round and round in an endless parade of color, the magical music of the calliope filled the air. It was enough to make Momma forget about her worries, if only for a short while. For the older kids, the best ride in the amusement park was the tilt-a-whirl ride. Each car spun around and around in circles as the whole ride rotated around and moved up and down. Shelby and Henry loved the ride but the younger ones were really too young to ride. Always looking for a good laugh, Shelby offered to pay for Maggie's ride if she would agree to ride with them. Of course, she would! It was not every day that Shelby and Henry actually wanted her to do something with them. Hmmm. Did that sound familiar? As soon as the ride started up, Maggie thought that maybe she had made a mistake. After two minutes of swirling around and being slammed this way and that way, she was sure of it. When the ride finally stopped and she was able to stagger off, she commenced to throwing up everything she had eaten not just today but yesterday too. In fact, she was sure she even saw a bit of last week's bologna sandwich.

Chapter 6
Doodle Bugs and Bee Stings

In August of 1966, Momma decided to take everyone on a road trip to visit her sister, Louise. It was an especially hot summer drive with no air conditioning in the car. Even though Shelby did not like to have her hair blown all about, the front windows were rolled down to let fresh air in. The back windows were rolled all the way up since the handles on both sides had broken. Aunt Louise lived about an hour away, near Lexington. She lived with her husband William in a little one-room house. The house was nothing extra, just a plain rectangle with raw wood plank siding. It did not even have any paint on it so it looked very much like the small pack house sitting next to the dirt path leading up to the house. The pack house was used to store the cured tobacco until it was packed and ready for market. Maggie loved to play near the pack house because the smell of cured tobacco was everywhere. It smelled so sweet, just like Momma's Honeybee snuff.

Tobacco was a popular cash crop in many southern states and the older kids had already had some experience working in tobacco although their experience was mostly with picking up leaves. They had not acquired much experience in actually looping tobacco yet so they liked to practice whenever they got the chance. A visit to Aunt Louise's house provided just such an opportunity. They gathered some old tobacco sticks, ones that were broken or splintered and headed down the dirt path leading to the paved road. To one side of the pack house stood an old dilapidated shed. This was the perfect place for them to practice looping their tobacco. Actually, their tobacco was nothing more than big-leaf weeds that grew wild in the sand. That didn't mater though; the principle was still the same.

Normally, the tobacco stick would be mounted atop a looping horse but, since they didn't have a looping horse, they had to improvise. They looked for a hole in the wall or even two planks on the wall with ample space between them; anything to hold the stick horizontally while the tobacco leaves were loaded. Luckily, the old shed had two holes in the wall perfect for holding their sticks snugly. After tying the tobacco twine at the far end of the stick, Henry held the twine with his left hand while holding a small bundle of tobacco leaves, usually three or four, with his right hand. After laying the tobacco on the twine, the twine was wrapped completely around it. The tobacco was then pushed all the way to the far end of the stick so it hung down the right side. The next bundle was strung in the same manner except that this bundle was pushed to the end of the stick and then flipped over the top of the stick so that the tobacco hung down on the left side. Henry repeated this process until the stick was completely full of raw, green tobacco. Over time, all the children took turns and in just a short while, they were all proficient loopers. Then they practiced "taking off" the tobacco and packing it just like the farmers did before taking it to market to sell. These newfound talents would most definitely come in handy when they were old enough to work as loopers for one of the tobacco farmers around home.

With all the tobacco barns and pack houses nearby, Aunt Louise had probably the best and biggest doodlebugs around and all the kids spent countless hours searching for them. Doodlebugs were easy to spot as they hid mostly in the sand under tobacco barn shelters or porches. Their homes looked like upside down anthills, making funnels into the sand. The good thing about doodlebugs was that anyone could dig for them and everyone could do it together, all at the same time. In fact, the more, the merrier. First, each person would pull a straw from the kitchen broom. About four inches was enough but most of the time, the straw that broke loose would be at least six or eight inches long. This was quite alright too because broom straws are great to chew on and pick your teeth with so naturally, the best thing to do would be to break off the excess straw and put in your mouth, off to the side so it would not interfere with you speaking. Then the actual digging for doodlebugs began. The proper technique is to stick the broom straw into the middle of the sand funnel, holding it in a perfectly vertical position. While "stirring" the straw, that is moving the straw in a clockwise circular motion, you would repeat these words: "Doodlebug, doodlebug, come out of that hole. Doodlebug, doodlebug, come out of that hole." The phrase had to be repeated during the whole stirring process until the doodlebug came out of the hole or attached itself to the straw. Once captured, the doodlebug was added to the growing collection of doodlebugs kept in a Mason jar filled half-way with sand. It was always amazing to watch as the bugs scooted backwards, pinchers working back and forth frantically, trying to get back underneath to the safety of the sand. Even more exciting was putting a few doodlebugs in your hand and letting them scoot all around. Sure, they had pinchers but they didn't pinch, only tickle.

As good as Maggie, Bethany and Sarah loved doodlebug collecting; eventually they wanted to be where their older brother and sister were. If they were left behind, they made it their mission to find the others and be with them, whether the older kids liked it or not. On this particular day, Aunt Louise had just gotten home from the dime store and had brought all the young'uns a special treat. The plain brown dime store bag was filled to the top with candy wax. There were lips and harmonicas and soda-shaped bottles, all made from the specially flavored wax. This was indeed a surprise for the children did not receive frivolous and unnecessary things very often. Shelby and Henry took their treats and headed off into the woods while the younger three children took theirs and sat down in the sand to play with Aunt Louise's new puppies. They had just been born the week before, underneath one of the pack houses.

Evening was just beginning to take over the bright, sunny day and, as the evening sounds began to grow increasingly louder, lightning bugs started to flicker here and there. As Sarah played contentedly with the puppies, Bethany and Maggie became restless and decided that they would go find the big kids and ask them to help catch some lightning bugs to go in their lightning bug lantern. They had just made the lantern the day before from a mason jar. They had poked holes in the tin lid and wrapped a wire around the top for the handle. Because they were, after all, "just as big" as the others, they started in the direction they had seen Shelby and Henry go.

They walked along the old timber road, dragging tobacco sticks behind them with one hand and holding the lightening bug lantern with the other. They took special care to avoid the sandspurs that grew like wildfire in this sandy area. As they walked farther and farther away from the safety of Aunt Louise's house, they could hear voices through the trees and, with the light fading fast, decided to go straight through the woods rather than stay on the well worn path.

It took less than five minutes for them to find major trouble. They had not found the others but they had definitely found something; something very, very bad. Without seeing it, they had unknowingly walked right into a hornet's nest, literally. It was nestled just to one side of the very route they had chosen to follow. When Shelby and Henry heard all the screaming and carrying on, they quickly came to the rescue, but then they always did. Shelby immediately commenced to stripping off Bethany and Maggie's clothes, for the hornets had somehow managed to find their way in and were still stinging—under arms and around necks and legs, around eyes and ears, absolutely everywhere. It was a sight to behold as the two sisters, accompanied by their rescuers, returned to Aunt Louise's, not much older but definitely much wiser. By the time Momma and Aunt Louise had finished with their doctoring, the two girls were as brown as the inside of a spittoon. That was not surprising, considering. You see, everyone in these parts knew that tobacco juice was a very effective treatment for any kind of insect sting. Momma had made a paste of snuff and water and had smeared it all over both girls' bodies; that is, all except their eyes which stayed swollen shut for two days. Maggie and Bethany learned real quick that sometimes it is better to be left behind.

Chapter 7
School Daze and Dime Stores

Even when school was out, the Leonard children loved to play school, especially Shelby who made a very good teacher. Shelby had her "school" set up in the bedroom that she and Maggie shared with Henry. It was complete with chalkboard, a small chalkboard that is. She taught English, Math and Music. Shelby even had a ruler she used to smack hands if someone got out of line or did not work to their full potential. On the brighter side though, in August, they took a school holiday when it was Elvis' birthday because he was one of Shelby's favorites. Shelby even taught the kids to sing and dance to *Blue Christmas* when December rolled around.

The fall of 1965 was an exciting time for Maggie as she was finally old enough to start school. Sure, she had attended Shelby's school but now she could finally go to real school. She already knew how to spell and write her name and she was anxious to show the teacher how smart she was.

Before the school year commenced, it was necessary to make sure she was up to date on all of her immunization shots. It wasn't often that Maggie got to spend time alone, just her and Momma, but today was special. She and Momma took the afternoon and headed to the health department. No one had forewarned Maggie about the shots she was to get and she was quite taken aback when she saw the nurse come in with two needles. As the nurse jabbed them carelessly, first one into her arm and then the second one into her thigh, Maggie sat helplessly, wincing in pain though she tried hard not to. The lollipop offered after the assault did not help nor did the kisses that Momma planted on the wounded body parts. Maggie felt totally betrayed. It was a betrayal of great magnitude for her own momma to take her, an unsuspecting child, to such a place to be hurt like that. As they made their way from the clinic to the dime store, however, the pain was quickly forgotten. It sure is amazing how such a small thing as a new pair of flip-flops can completely erase such a seemingly devastating hurt.

Birthdays were always special in the Leonard household. Momma always went the extra mile to make sure no one felt left out. Sure, the birthday kid got a birthday cake and a special little something more, but everyone else got something too, just not as big. Not that any of the gifts were big. They were mostly little stuffed animals Momma had picked up from the dime store. The small, sawdust-filled toys were simply tokens, reminders of Momma's love. And that was enough.

On rare occasions, Maggie and her brother and sisters would all pile into the car and go with Momma to the dime store. Just to go to town was a treat in itself. The grocery store or the Sears catalog store was fine but the dime store, well that was something extraordinary. The dime store was the one place where kids could shop, even if they did not have much money. Because there wasn't a lot of extra money, everyone saved their pennies and nickels and waited, anticipating the day when the family could take a much anticipated trip to the dime store. Money was earned occasionally by working for one of the local farmers picking up tobacco leaves around the barns as the tobacco was being looped and hung for curing. The farmers paid twenty-five cents per day for each child who worked hard.

The kids were not aware of exactly how far it was or how long it would take to get to the dime store, but as they got closer and closer, somehow they could sense the nearness and, with each turn of the road, the excitement and anticipation grew.

Once inside the store, each Leonard kid, with a few coins in hand, would carefully walk up and down each aisle, scoping out every possibility. The smell of popcorn and new plastic filled their nostrils as they walked up and down the hardwood floors. There was not a better smell in the world. They went back and forth, back and forth. Among the goodies that could be found at the dime store were the usual assortment of glass piggy banks, blue and pink flocked bunny banks, slinkies, flip-flops and such. The store also had lots of their all time favorites—marbles, jack rocks, baseballs and badminton.

Since Shelby liked to play school, she could usually find something desireable in the section reserved for stationary and school supplies.

Henry first liked to look at the comic books. Of course, he never bought them because he was thrifty and had decided to save his pennies for something really, really special. Just what, he did not know just yet. As always, he eventually found his way to the hardware and handyman section. Spools of wire, kite string, building supplies and tools. That was the kind of stuff that he almost always wound up buying, he being the inventor type that he was.

At the front of the store was a counter where penny candy was stuffed tightly into rows and rows of funny shaped glass jars sealed with corked-rimmed tops. Some of the jars even had the kind of lids that had the metal arm that swung over the top to hold them tightly in place. Maggie's favorite candy was squirrel nut zippers. She usually purchased at least a couple of the chewy caramel and nut treats along with a few BB Bats and peanut butter Mary Janes. Bethany and Sarah also loved the penny candy counter and each one always seemed to make a point of going home with a nickels' worth of sweets every time. That way, if they could manage it, they could have a piece for each of the next few days. They were younger than the rest and not particularly interested in the other things the store had to offer but candy was always a big hit with them.

At the end of the shopping spree, everyone would load back up into the car, scrunched shoulder to shoulder and sometimes stacked two high if they decided to lie down. As Momma made the turn at the edge of town, she looked in her rear-view mirror to catch a glimpse of her children sleeping, each with a smile as big as all of Texas.

During the days way before the school system was desegregated; all the school-aged Leonards attended the same school—Clancey School. It was just a few miles from home but the daily bus trip carried them right through Black Swamp. Two miles of the scariest road in the county, they had built it through the middle of a swamp with trees that reached right out over the pavement. The moss hung low, until it seemingly encompassed and hid the road from the sun. That made for a shady ride on hot, sunny days but at the same time, created an eerie, almost creepy feeling when traveling down this dark, shadowed path. The ditches on either side seemed to stretch out forever into the adjacent woods making it possible for any wood creatures to have easy access to the road and its unsuspecting travelers. Luckily, the only animals spotted so far were turtles, rabbits, snakes and squirrels. Still, other things *could* have been lurking just beyond sight. You could never be quite sure.

Just when you thought you might never make it out of the dark, eerie tree tunnel, you'd reach the far end and sunlight would burst through the trees and hope would be restored. At the edge of the swamp, just before Clancey School came into sight, there was a spring, a natural spring. Long ago, someone had cleared the area and stuck a pipe in the ground making it easy to get a cool drink, straight from the ground. Through the years, this had become a unique place to stop, not just for locals but also for visitors passing through the area.

Shelby, being the oldest, had arrived at the point in her life where hair had become very important. She was constantly trying new hairstyles. She had very straight, dark hair and wished it could be a little curlier. But then, the grass is always greener…On one of the family's trips to the dime store, Shelby purchased a set of spongy, foam rollers. She had heard from some of the girls at school that sponge rollers would give a curl to even the straightest hair. These rollers were soft and pink and Shelby thought they would work nicely. Each one had a plastic rod running through the middle of the foam with a stretchy thingy attached to one end with a clip to hook it to the other end. They probably would even be comfortable to sleep in.

Now at Shelby's age, she just could not take a chance with her own hair, at least not the very first time. What would she do if it did not turn out just right? Maybe too curly or curly just on one side and not on the other? She would not get to wash it out until next Saturday. She decided to include Maggie once again in her grand experiment. That was just fine with Maggie as she loved to be included in big girl things. Besides, her hair had always been straight as a stick and she, too, wanted a little curl. As luck would have it, the curlers were very comfortable and did not keep Maggie from getting her full eight hours.

When the morning came, Shelby quickly began taking curlers out but Maggie's long hair tended to get tangled and it seemed to take practically forever. By the time all the curlers were out, it was time for the bus to come. Shelby ran the hairbrush through Maggie's hair one quick time before zipping out the door to get on the bus. Everyone else was already on board and calling for Maggie to hurry so, as she ran, the thought did not occur to her that her hair might not be simply beautiful. Her sister certainly would not do that to her. Would she?

As soon as she took her seat on the bus, the snickers started, low at first then grew louder. Once at school, Maggie headed straight for the restroom where she could visually inspect her special "doo." Obviously, the curlers did their job without exemption. The curls might not have been so bad if Maggie had not been only six years old and in the first grade. Naturally, she did not know that just a few years before, Shirley Temple was being paid to have her hair look this very way.

Chapter 8
Rub a Dub

Saturday was work day, set aside for cleaning house and washing laundry. It did not take all day but it did take a good portion of the day. As you might expect, all of the kids had chores around the house.

Bethany and Sarah's primary job was to not get in the way and they were extremely good at it. As they sat on the back porch playing jacks, Henry cut and split wood and stacked it. The wood would be needed later for the wood stove. Cutting and splitting wood was a vital job but it was hard work too. The good news was that it helped build muscles and muscles are something that young men can never have too many of.

Shelby helped Momma clean the inside of the house. First, they would sweep all the floors and then mop them. The mopping went fairly quickly with their system, especially in the kitchen. They put pine sol and water in an aluminum bucket then simply poured it on the floor a little at a time. A few swishes with the mop and they were ready to rinse. The real trick was to try to swish over the whole floor before all of the water ran downhill and seeped out the holes under the wall. You see, the floors and the bottom of the walls were already partially rotten from the recurring flooding of the creek that ran along the back side of the property. It seemed like that that old creek flooded every five years or so. There was no vacuuming since there were no carpets, only vinyl. There was no bathroom to clean so the only things left were dusting and cleaning the stove.

The old wringer washing machine was legendary for making a wet mess on the floor, too. Even if there had been room inside the house for the washer, there was no need to compound the floor-rot problem so laundry was relegated to the back porch. Maggie's job was to help with the laundry. She liked pulling the soaking wet clothes from the washtub and feeding them into the wringer. After they came out of the wringer, it only took a short while on the clothesline for them to completely dry. Shelby used to help with the laundry until the wringer sucked up her arm, clean to the elbow. After that, she traded her laundry assignment for mopping the kitchen floor and cleaning the oven. On a lucky Saturday, the concrete porch would remain dry, thereby saving Maggie and the others from the shock that inevitably came from something not being properly grounded. Once the laundry was dry, Bethany and Sarah helped to fold the small things, as best they could.

At the end of the day, after all of the laundry had been washed, hung out to dry and taken in, it was time to drag the galvanized tub onto the back porch. The porch was screened-in and, even though there were plenty of holes in the screen, it still helped to keep the mosquitoes, bugs and snakes out. Water was pumped from the spigot, heated on the stove in Grandma's big, black canning pot and then added to the tub. When the water level was sufficient for bathing, everyone was shooed inside and the kids were sent back out, two at a time, to take a bath. Two at the time, that is, except for Henry. Being the only boy, he got to bathe alone, lucky guy.

Sunday was always considered a day of rest and family time. After Sunday school, preaching and dinner was over, all the kids would scoot outside to play together. After the chores from the previous day, they were more than ready to have some fun. Among their favorite things to do was making "rice krispies." It wasn't always a simple task though. First, they would have to sneak a cup or so of plain white rice from the pie safe cupboard in the kitchen. Then they would go out to Grandma's garage apartment and use her wood stove to cook the rice treat. Of course, Grandma was not there since she was living in the house now. She definitely would not have liked them wasting food like that. The easy part was stoking the fire with wood. After the stove was hot enough, they would put in a bit of lard to grease up the bottom of the iron frying pan. Once the pan was good and hot, it didn't take long at all for the rice to start popping. Even though the homemade rice krispies were distinctly different; that is to say, not quite as tasty as the stored-bought cereal, it was a great treat nonetheless. Sometimes, if the rice got a bit too done or the flavor was not quite right, they would just pop a handful into their mouths and play machine gun, seeing who could "shoot" the farthest.

All the children liked to play and work together. That is just how things were done at their house. That was never more true than the day that Shelby decided that it would be a great idea to do something nice for Momma by painting the outside of the house. The house, with its grey cinder block exterior, certainly could use a facelift. The only paint that could be found around the house was the pepto bismal pink paint that had been used to paint Momma's bedroom the year before. They had gotten it on sale and, though the color might have been just a bit bright, they did not really mind. In fact, they loved bright colors. Therefore, Shelby and the others painted the house pepto bismal pink, but only on one side. There was no more paint after that; they had used all they had. Momma was indeed surprised beyond words when she arrived home that day.

Chapter 9
Halloween and Christmas in Dixie

Maggie and her family lived in a rural area. That meant that the houses were few and far between. The closest neighbors were the Marvins and they lived about a quarter mile up the road. That might seem pretty close but the Marvins did not celebrate or promote Halloween. They had no children living at home and to them, Halloween was a heathen holiday anyway. Translated, there would be no trick or treating at their house. Though Momma did not condone *begging*, this one day of the year she did allow dressing up and trick-or-treating. There were no such things as store-bought costumes so everyone dressed up in whatever they could find around the house. Usually, they'd create a couple of pirates by tying a piece of scrap fabric around the head and darkening their eyes and faces with soot from the woodstove. Princesses or mommies were even easier because only a dress was required. One year, there was even a ghost since one of the sheets had become so ragged, it was no longer usable.

A couple of eye holes and—ta da—a ghost. Once everyone was dressed, they collected their pillowcases and Momma drove them to town where they could walk down the city sidewalks and trick-or-treat quickly and safely. Once in a while they encountered a ghost or ghoul that gave tricks instead of treats. One time they were even met at the door by a grey man with a water spigot attached to his forehead. He even turned the handle and water poured out! As one might expect, the kids did not wait to see if treats would be offered. Terrified, they quickly dashed across the street to safety. Just as they reached the sidewalk on the opposite side of the street, they heard the sound of laughter and then the sound of candy hitting the ground as the grey man began throwing it over to them. Little bags of candy corn—their favorite! Old faucet face wasn't so bad after all.

Christmas was always a particularly special time at the Leonard home. They were poor but they did not know it. When Momma pulled out the shiny silver aluminum Christmas tree, everyone gathered around excitedly to help set it up. Each separate tinsel limb had to be carefully removed from the protective paper sleeve and inserted into the center pole. After the tree was completely assembled, it was decorated with strings of red, yellow, green, orange and blue lights and then strung with paper chains and popcorn. The final touch was the addition of the carefully stored, fragile glass ornaments that had been in the family for several decades. Christmas spirit and love filled the house as Momma and Henry nailed pillowcases, one for each child, around the door facing. They didn't have Christmas stockings; in fact, they didn't know anyone who did; so the pillowcases were used to hold whatever goodies Santa might bring. Paper dolls and coloring books were the normal fare for the younger girls; posters or freshly sewn dresses for the older girls; a cap gun or slingshot for Henry.

Add these items to the few pieces of fruit and nuts that the neighbors sometimes dropped off and you had the recipe for a perfect Christmas. As far as the Leonard children knew, this is what everybody got for Christmas.

On Christmas Eve, 1965, just about dusk, it started to snow. As everyone excitedly ran to look out the window, Henry stumbled and fell, knocking the Christmas tree over, breaking a windowpane in the process. Even though the air pouring in was freezing cold, there was no way it could dampen the warmth and love that this family felt at this most special time of the year.

Chapter 10
Hero

One day, just as spring was beginning to break winter's hold and the yellow daffodils were just commencing to force their way up through the ground, a special report came on television. The television reporter was excitedly announcing the arrival of a group of soldiers back home to Fort Jackson. Maggie sat, watching as the events unfolded on the small black and white television set. The reception was not very good, but Henry wiggled and jiggled the flimsy antenna until at last they were able to catch a glimpse of the soldiers. The uniforms they wore made them all look handsome and the perfect precision with which they marched seemed to magnify their dignity and honor. Maggie sat, admiring these men who had put their lives on the line.

There had been a lot of talk about the war amongst the old men down at the gas station. It seemed as if these same conversations had been going on forever. Was this war really necessary and was it doing any good? Too, there was much debate about the president's decisions lately. Before seeing all this recent stuff on the television, Maggie had thought that being the President of the United States was a glamorous job but now, she wasn't so sure. She began to think that being a president must be quite a bit like being a parent. Her younger sister, Bethany, had just finished a school project entitled, "George Washington, Father of Our Country." Boy, what a big family! Maggie could imagine how tough it would be making decisions that would affect many, many people. Then, what if others did not agree with you? At the same time, she realized that the President and his assistants probably had access to information that everyday folks did not, and that put them in a better position to plan things and make major decisions. She finally decided to put her trust in her President because she knew in her heart that he would make the best decision he could, based on the information he had. At least she hoped so.

As she watched the soldiers reuniting with their loved ones, Maggie thought how proud they all looked; the soldiers proud of their jobs and their families proud of them. Maggie wished she could be proud of her uncle Gerald. He had been in the Army and had returned home from Vietnam only a few months before. He certainly did not act like the soldiers on television; in fact, just the opposite. There was always tension in the air when Gerald was around and that made everyone uneasy. Whenever he came for a visit, the air would become so thick with his malice and hatefulness, he absolutely sucked the joy and happiness right out of everyone, even his own wife. He was arrogant and abusive and disrespected everyone, but most especially women. In spite of his attitude toward others, Gerald felt entitled to their admiration and if he did not get it, he would sooner slap them as to look at them.

The last time Gerald visited, Maggie, along with all the other children, tried to find out-of-the way places to hide so he would not see them. They had taken to doing this every time he visited. On this particular day, Maggie did not have enough time to find a good hideout and decided to crawl under the kitchen table. Surely, the six chairs tucked under the table would be enough to shield her. Wrong! Gerald spotted her as soon as he walked through the doorway and called impatiently for her to come out. Cautiously and silently, Maggie came out. She did not wish to have a conversation nor confrontation with Gerald. After her continued silence and repeated failure to answer his questions, he announced that he would start calling her "Silent Sam." When he asked if she would like that, Maggie replied simply, "No." Gerald demanded that she show a little respect and address him as "sir" but no matter how he yelled, Maggie did not respect him and would not call him "sir." In a fit of rage, Gerald slapped her across the face so hard that she fell back against the kitchen table, hitting her back on the table corner. Shelby was always the one to try and protect the younger ones whenever Momma was not around and, when she heard the commotion, she ran in from the back yard. The slam of the screen door temporarily distracted Gerald, giving Maggie just enough time to run out, thereby escaping further abuse. She was crying and hurt, but in her mind, she had won. She had shown Gerald that he could not demand respect and he could not beat it out of her. He would have to earn it, just like everyone else.

Even though she kept many of her thoughts to herself, Maggie was very observant and insightful well beyond her years. She was well aware that, of Grandma's three children, Gerald was her favorite. Was it because he was the oldest? Maybe. Or maybe it was simply because he was her only male child. Whatever the reason, it was as clear as the day was long that Grandma loved him more than she loved Momma. Even when he stole Momma's car. Even when he took Henry's bicycle and ran it off the bridge and into the river. Yes, it was very clear that Gerald was Grandma's favorite. About that, there was never any question.

In the summer of 1966, Gerald and his wife, Rebecca, announced the arrival of a new baby, a baby boy. Grandma had never been much of a baby person but she was certainly quick enough to volunteer Shelby for diaper duty. Shelby had to go stay with them for a few days to help out until things settled down. On Labor Day Monday, Shelby returned home. As usual, all the children tried to make themselves scarce as soon as they heard the loud roar of the approaching car. Maggie crouched behind the large wisteria bush next to the house, its cascading, purple, flowery tentacles hiding her from view. That is how it happened that she found out just how truly hurtful this uncle could be. She realized at that point that she had not been singled out; no, he was equally vicious to everyone he came in contact with.

When Shelby got out of the car, Maggie noticed right away that she was not her usual good-humored self. The sparkle had gone right out of her hazel eyes and underneath she had dark circles that made her look a bit like a zombie. She walked somewhat slowly, like someone who had just hoed a whole garden of summer corn by herself. Maggie closed her eyes, wishing herself invisible, as Gerald grabbed Shelby by the arm, adding to the already black and blue places above her elbow, and commenced to beating her. Again. This time, he used her very own hairbrush, forcing the sharp bristles deep into her back and legs, cursing all the while and daring her to cry or yell for help.

Since returning from the war, Gerald had become a drunk. As nasty as he was sober, he was twice as bad after he had been

67

drinking. Maggie thought he must have been mad at God and everybody else because of the war and then on top of all that, his new son had been born special. The old people called it *special* but Maggie knew that special was just a polite way of saying mentally retarded.

The last few months had been tough ones for everyone but most especially for Momma. Jobs were hard to find and even harder to keep so when the opportunity came to rent a small house near her sister Louise, Momma jumped at it. At least staying at White Ridge, Louise would be able to help watch the kids while Momma looked for work. It was while staying here, away from the comfort of their family home, that Maggie found out first hand the true meaning of the word hero.

Henry had been asking for a shotgun of his own for quite some time. Though he was a tad small for his age, he still insisted that he was old enough, and big enough, to handle a gun. He wanted to go rabbit hunting and squirrel hunting. He was particularly interested in hunting down some of those big snapping turtles that lived near the creek in the woods back home. The old folks called them "cooters." They were good eating; tasted just like chicken but then, so did alligator. Anyway, when Henry woke up that Christmas morning in 1966, he found a shotgun, the very one he had been eyeing in the Western Auto catalog. As Henry scooped up the magical gift from its resting place in the corner behind the Christmas tree, you could not have found a happier boy in all of South Carolina.

Technically, winter had begun only the week before but already it had been a harsh one. It was so cold in fact, that after three days of non-stop snowfall; the water pump had frozen solid. In order to have water for cooking, Momma sent Henry and Maggie out to collect buckets of fresh snow from the top of the car and anywhere else they could. Now, as Henry stood there in the front yard, snow bucket in hand, he spotted Gerald's rust bucket of a car sliding up the snow-covered dirt road. Henry anticipated that trouble would be following close behind; it always did. Expecting no less this time, Henry snuck back into the house and headed straight for his new gun. He then waited, crouching out of sight behind the couch, his gun tucked tightly under his arm. As always, Gerald had been drinking and that meant he had come for one reason and one reason only; to take Momma's hard-earned money. If she had no money, he took whatever he could find that he might be able to pawn for a few bucks.

Momma had always been a giver, one who would help anyone in need and she would have gladly given Gerald what she could spare. Since Daddy died, Lord knows she had been forced to depend on the kindness of others herself more than once. With five children, and it being Christmas time and all, she barely had money enough to make her own ends meet, much less money to spare. She definitely did not have extra money for Gerald to buy whiskey and cigarettes, especially since he had not hit a lick since getting out of the Army.

Momma explained her situation and sorrow at not being able to offer assistance, and sure enough, true to form, Gerald, without missing a beat, lit into her like a raving lunatic. Momma had been much weaker lately, probably her kidneys acting up again, and now, when she needed strength to defend herself, she had none. Nor was she able to have a rational discussion with her brother. Gerald was busy, his attention totally focused on dragging Momma out the door by her hair. Just then, Henry quickly and quietly slipped up behind him, shotgun in hand, standing taller and straighter than any soldier Maggie had ever seen on the television. Just as Gerald was about to succeed in forcing Momma to hand over her pocketbook, Henry stuck the cold, hard barrel of the gun to Gerald's back and, with the biggest, loudest voice his eleven-year-old body could muster, yelled, "You bastard, leave my Momma alone or I will kill you dead right where you stand!" Although Gerald had been in Vietnam and probably encountered hand-to-hand combat, he could tell that Henry was not bluffing and meant exactly what he was saying. In fact, Gerald had never heard Henry use that tone before. He knew right then, without giving a second thought, that the wise choice, no the only choice, would be to retreat. Immediately!

Maggie, hiding under the kitchen table, as had become her custom, was sick with fear and yet, at the same time, was filled with pride clean up to her eyeballs. Her brother Henry had just become a hero, not just to her, but to the whole entire family, braver than any of the soldiers Maggie had seen on the television just weeks before.

.

PART II

THE END
OF THE
BEGINNING

Chapter 11
Friends and Family

Momma was not well educated nor was she a social butterfly. She had graduated from the eighth grade which was actually quite advanced for the 1940's. That was the same for most of her kinfolk, especially the females, and that was about all that one could expect in Marlboro County where she grew up. In any case, everyone in the Clancey community, where she had made her home since her marriage to Walter, liked and respected her. They especially admired her courage under dismal circumstances. Lord knows, she had gone through some very trying times, especially since Walter's death. Fact was, she had been forced to survive for her family's sake.

Momma had always been a hard worker. She placed a high value on honesty and integrity and always tried to set a good example for her children. Nowadays, her world consisted of going to work at the shirt factory at six thirty every morning, working eight hours making minimum wage, then coming home and taking care of her five children, her mother and her home. After supper, Momma spent many long evenings cutting out material and sewing clothes for the children. She was especially good at transforming flour sacks and chicken feed sacks into beautiful dresses and shorts. She was always careful when making her chicken feed purchases, taking extra care to choose the sacks with the prettiest patterns. After skillfully measuring and drawing individual patterns for each child, she would send the children off to bed where they drifted off to sleep many nights to the soothing sound of Momma's Singer peddle sewing machine. Occasionally, they would stay up well past their bedtime and help her sew by working the sewing machine peddle back and forth while she maneuvered the fabric underneath the pressure foot. Undoubtedly, Momma could have probably made more headway without their help but she never minded since it meant she could spend a bit more time with them.

Ever so slowly, over time, Momma had begun to get her life back together. She still missed her beloved Walter. He was her first love and a day never passed that she did not long to touch him or speak to him about the everyday things. However, she was not one to dwell indefinitely in the past and finally she decided, almost unconsciously, that the time had come to move forward. It would not be easy putting the past behind her but it would be the best thing she could do for her children. She never talked too much about the sadness that seemed to linger at times for she, like any good mother, tried to protect her children from life and the bad that it sometimes threw in the way. Even so, Maggie and Shelby knew. Even at a very young age, they could tell by Momma's actions, the far away looks and the unexplained quietness that sometimes came over her, that in fact, their momma was not quite as ready for the future as she would like to believe.

Many of the neighbors, knowing how very difficult it must be to make ends meet, made a special effort to help as much as they could, whenever they could. Mr. Murphy had bought a store just a ways up the road from the house and would often times stop by to see if there were soft drink bottles that needed to be returned for the deposit. The deposit was only five cents per bottle, but five cents is five cents. A bottle here and a bottle there and before long, you're talking about some real money. Though there were never very many, he happily picked them up anyway. While he was there, he would usually just happen to have a few extra cans of peas or tomatoes he didn't need. Once in while, if there were a few extra dollars, Momma would send Henry to Mr. Murphy's store to pick up some bologna or candy. The store, about a mile from the house, was a good walk for him, but he never complained. It was actually quite an honor to be depended on and to have a part in taking care of the family. After all, he was the man of the house now.

The times of having store-bought treats were few and far in between. Mostly, the supper menu consisted of store-bought rice served with vegetables from the garden—tomatoes, corn, okra, colored butterbeans, field peas, string beans or squash. Bread, of course, was cooked every day because it was both filling and relatively inexpensive. Sometimes, cornbread was baked and sometimes flour bread was fried but the best bread was Grandma's hand-squished cat head biscuits. They were called cat head biscuits because that is how big they were, as big as a cat's head. They were as big as a hand and high as a fist. They were everyone's favorite, better than flour bread or cornbread. The best way to enjoy one of these monster biscuits was to stick a finger in the top and then bend it while turning the biscuit. This made a hollow in the middle for such sweet goodness as molasses or corn syrup. Grandma Moses' Molasses was the best. It was always a race to see who could hollow out their biscuit first. Most times, the children drank water with their supper and the grownups drank tea. Every week or two, Momma allowed everyone to have a Coke as a special treat.

During the summer months, Momma and Grandma worked the garden so they could freeze and can as many vegetables as possible. This made for extra long days, especially for Momma on days when she had already worked a full shift at the shirt factory. They did it dutifully, though, because they knew that when the canned and frozen foods ran out, it was back to store-bought canned tomatoes and rice until the next gardening season rolled around. As was the case with many things in this family, all of the children who were old enough helped out by shelling peas, shucking corn, snapping beans; whatever was needed.

Momma and Daddy had bought their small piece of land from Mr. Marvin when they first moved to the area. The Marvins, living on the adjacent farm, had seen the family grow from the very beginning. They had been there for Momma at the birth of each of her children as well as at the death of her third child, Edward. Most recently, they had been there with Momma when Sarah arrived, just seven short months after Walter's death. Mr. and Mrs. Marvin were much older and they took a grandparent-like interest in the kids since their own children lived far away.

The Marvins were among the first in the area to get a telephone in their home as they were better off financially than many of the families. Grandma did not know how, nor did she want to know how to use the telephone, but she or Momma would, from time to time, need to send a message and would have Shelby or Henry go to the Marvin's to make the call for them. Once, Maggie and Bethany went to borrow a cup of sugar from Mrs. Marvin so they could help Shelby make a birthday cake for Momma. The

Marvins always seemed to have whatever was needed, no matter what it was, and were always willing to share.

The only thing between the two houses was a section of woods and a good-sized cow pasture. Highway 176 was not typically a busy road, though at times, traffic tended to nudge the fifty-five mile per hour speed limit. For this reason, Momma did not like the kids to be on the road, even for the short quarter mile. She preferred that they hike through the woods and around the cow pasture. The kids, being kids, usually took a short-cut through the cow pasture rather than walk around it. There had never been a problem; that is until Mr. Marvin bought a bull. For the most part, the bull ignored the children as they slipped through the corner of his pen. It was not easy hurrying while trying to be careful not to get hung up on the barbed wire and the electric fence. Occasionally though, the bull would catch sight of a red shirt or skirt and go temporarily a little nuts. God must have been looking out for the children as they never did get into any real trouble with the bull. That's not to say, however, that each and every crossing was not an exhilarating experience.

When Sunday morning rolled around, Mr. and Mrs. Marvin would always stop by on their way to church. Mt. Herman Church, just about five or so miles toward town, provided a wonderful Sunday school for children and had many, many attending. The Marvins regularly picked up at least two or three children. Momma stayed at home. She already knew God and preferred to talk to him at home. Still, she wanted each of her children to get to know and understand Him and the valuable lessons that Sunday school taught so she allowed them to go each week with the Marvins. Of course, since Bethany and Maggie shared Sunday dresses and shoes, they had to take turns.

When Momma and Daddy first moved to Clancey, they met Robert and Joann Graham. The Grahams had always lived in the area and were eager to help them get settled in. Even after Daddy died, the Grahams had remained among Momma's closest friends. God had not blessed Robert and Joann with children of their own so that made them even more drawn to the expansive brood. It was quite natural for them to visit, oftentimes bringing small gifts. While the Grahams loved all the children, they had fallen in love particularly with Maggie, the middle child. She was what they called the pick of the litter with her clear blue eyes and corn silk colored hair.

The Grahams could see how difficult it was at times for Momma to keep her family going and on several occasions had even offered to have Maggie come live with them. In fact, they adored her so much they had made the same offer several times through the years, even before Daddy died and the hard times had become a normal part of their lives. While Momma's heart truly ached for her childless friends, she simply could not part with her sweet, special Maggie. Because the Grahams knew how special Maggie was, they completely understood and quietly agreed to go on being Uncle Rob and Aunt Jo. They certainly spoiled the children just like an aunt and uncle would. Aunt Jo worked in town at one of the sewing factories and whenever the company had extra clothing samples, she would bring them to Shelby and Maggie. Uncle Rob, though a quiet man, occasionally spent time with Henry, talking and laughing and even taking him fishing at one of the ponds on his farm. During the tobacco season, Uncle Rob offered jobs to Henry, Shelby, Maggie and Grandma and on occasion, even allowed Bethany and Sarah to help. To the area tobacco farmers, even the younger children proved to be good workers during a busy season.

In the opposite direction, the Wilson family lived about a mile away with their four boys who were around the same ages as Shelby and Henry. Every once in a while, a bag of fruit would appear on the front porch, always anonymously. Momma always knew that it had been the Wilsons who had sent the fruit and she was always grateful for their thoughtfulness and generosity. It was also common knowledge, at least to Maggie and Henry, that the Wilsons also played Santa at Christmas by leaving boxes of assorted fruits and nuts on the doorstep. No one lived up to the motto "It's more blessed to give than receive" than the Wilson family did. Momma and her children were truly blessed to have such wonderful and loving neighbors.

Momma had always been close to her sister, Louise. In reality, they were only half-sisters since they had the same mother but a different father. Of course, no one would ever have known it. No matter what happened, Louise was there for her. Just like the Marvins, the Grahams and the Wilsons, Louise had been there when baby Edward died and she had been there when Daddy died. Of course, Momma had always been there for Louise too, like when she got divorced from her first husband and when she remarried, became pregnant and then lost the baby. Momma and Louise were probably as close as two sisters could be. They had to be each other's support growing up, especially with them taking second and third place in the line waiting for affection from their mother. Now as grownups, Momma and Louise remained each other's very best friend and Louise helped as much as she could with the children even though she now lived in Richland County, a right far piece away.

Her Walter had been dead well over five years before Momma began to have the slightest inclination to be interested in dating again. Her first priority was, of course, her children but as time went on, the emptiness began to grow and create a void that her children could not fill. Though Momma never asked anyone out loud what they thought of the whole dating idea, Maggie knew she was thinking about it and that she probably wondered, too, what her Walter would think of it. Maggie knew this because every once in a while she would hear Momma humming that old song, "When it's My Time," a song that Daddy had sung all those many, many years ago. It had been a lifetime ago that Momma had last heard the song, but when she thought that no one was around to hear, she would find the words flowing through her mind as easily as if she had just read them. What usually started with her humming always ended with her softly singing the last few words. They went something like this:

Many streams of tears may flood your waking time
And when sleep comes, it's filled with dreams unkind
Though it seems uphill, still you'll make it through
You can face it all for I am there with you

When it's my time, I will simply slip away
And I'll wait for you up there by heaven's gate

As tomorrow turns into yesterday
And the loneliness replaces all the pain
May your heart find love again with someone new
Hearts were made for love and so I bid adieu

When it's my time, I will simply slip away
To your new love, I'm giving you away

Chapter 12
Blind Love

Shelby was the oldest child and a middle-aged teenager. Though she was very sensitive to Momma's feelings, she was also the biggest critic of any suitor that tried to lay claim to Momma's time. Momma's time, particularly time that had always, until recently, been devoted to her family, was precious and Shelby wanted to make sure Momma didn't waste it on an unworthy gentleman caller. Then, too, it might just have been that Shelby was a little bit afraid of losing her mother, her confidant.

In the summer of 1967, a man entered their lives that seemed to be a perfect match. The mere mention of Richard's name brought a sparkle and shine to Momma's face. She grinned from ear to ear. That smile, that deep down, heart-felt smile had been missing for many, many years. Now she had a radiance about her that everyone noticed and, even though the children did not get to spend as much time alone with Momma as before, they were content. They thought that she had at last found someone who would love and take care of her. She had taken care of everyone else for so long and now, finally, it was her turn to be taken care of, to have a bit of happiness for herself.

Many, many years before, Momma and Daddy had been friends with Richard and his wife but had lost touch when Daddy died. With the family living in Calhoun County and Richard and his two sons living in Marlboro County, there really was not much opportunity to run into each other. That is why, in 1967, it was really quite a surprise to see Richard at the family reunion. It turned out that Richard's brother, John, had married one of the distant cousins only two years ago. Now, at the first reunion the family had held in about six years, John shows up with Richard and his children in tow. While John was a relative newlywed, Richard had been recently divorced.

When Richard and Momma met, it was as if the stars had aligned and everything was perfect again. Her world had been turned upside down for the past five years and now, for the first time since Daddy died, it looked as if the world was going to stop spinning and let her catch a ride on a shooting star. It's for sure that all the kids wished on every fallen star they saw. Momma probably did too. And now it seemed that maybe her wish had come true. She and Richard were immediately comfortable with each other and before long, were spending quite a bit of time together.

They courted, though in a somewhat unconventional manner. Sometimes Richard would come to Momma's house but most times Momma would load up all five kids and drive a good forty minutes over to Richard's house. Occasionally, Momma and Richard, wanting to spend some time alone, just the two of them, would leave all the kids together, with Shelby and Richard's oldest son, Chip, in charge. As the families spent more time together, they were able to tolerate each other but there was a clear division between the two groups of kids. Even someone who did not know them could have told the difference. Momma had raised her kids to be honest and caring but Richard's boys seemed to be not just rambunctious, but clearly scoundrels. Momma did not seem to notice, or at least she never said anything. She seemed as happy as the cat that got the canary. And why shouldn't she be? After all, she had found a man who doted on her and seemed willing to help her take care of her family.

Momma and Richard dated for several months and yet no one really suspected just how serious their relationship had become. Certainly, the children did not suspect. After all, even though they were of above average intelligence, they were still only children. Their minds were busy thinking on important things like doodlebugs, horseback riding and tree climbing. The seriousness of the situation finally became apparent to Maggie on Christmas morning in 1967. It had always been a tradition for all the kids to sleep together in one bedroom on Christmas Eve. That way, Santa could slip in, take care of his business and then slip back out totally unnoticed. On that Christmas morning, however, the kids awoke, not just to toys left by Santa, but also to the surprise of an extra person in the house. A man. Richard had spent the night and had even slept in Momma's bed. The wedding, if there had been one, had gone unannounced.

Chapter 13
The End

Chaos and tension grew with each moment since that night before when God had put out his hand and offered Momma release from the suffering she had been feeling since before the baby's arrival. At first, she fought back the notion of dying because she loved her children more than life itself and wanted to be with them, to take care and protect them. But after being reassured by Richard that he would make sure that her family was taken care of and kept safe, she quietly slipped her hand in God's as He lead her into the peacefulness that she longed for and deserved.

August 16, 1968; it was a Friday. Momma had been warned early on that her kidneys would not be able to withstand the pressure of repeated pregnancy. Still, she never considered any other alternative but to have the large family that she had always dreamed and yearned for. It was true that with each baby, her kidneys had grown weaker and weaker. Sure, there were times when the condition became somewhat transparent and went unnoticed. Still the damage was cumulative and so, in August 1968, just two days after the birth of her last child, a son, Momma returned to the hospital with uremia, a buildup of toxins resulting from kidney failure.

Children were not allowed in the hospital so, as Richard and Aunt Louise sat by Momma's bedside inside, the children, all five of them, waited outside in the car, alone in the dark. Not a word was heard for hours and hours and then, when the word did come, their world, as they had known it, collapsed. In the time it took to say those two words—she's gone—their world turned completely upside down. The poison had won and Momma was gone. Just three days ago, her thirty-sixth birthday had gone uncelebrated.

Momma's family and Richard's family fought, first over the baby and then over the funeral arrangements. Still, time moved on, for time waits for no man, or woman. Finally, on Monday, the funeral home brought Momma back home in a coffin set up in the living room, right where the old upright piano used to be. The coffin was a soft grey color. The material inside was light pink and satiny and reminded Maggie of being in a snuggly blanket. Momma looked peaceful at last as she lay with her slightly wavy, black hair neatly combed back. She wore a powder blue silky looking gown that Aunt Jo had given her. Before the appointed visiting hours, Aunt Louise took her Polaroid and snapped a picture of Momma, the last one ever to be taken. Maggie and the other children sat silently on the floor along the wall as friends, neighbors and strangers came and went. Some left food. Others simply came to pay their respects. No matter why they came or how long they stayed, it seemed to Maggie there was an awful lot of whispering. "Poor, poor children," she overheard them say.

"What's going to happen to them now?" Maggie wondered that very thing herself.

At the end of the day, the people from the funeral home came to take Momma's body back. August is a hot month—the dog days of summer and all—but August of 1968 was unusually hot. It would not have been a good idea at all to leave Momma's body at the house. At the funeral home, they would put her back in the cooler, with all of the other dead people, until the next day. Grandma and Aunt Louise announced that they would stay at the house but agreed with Richard that the children should be sent to his sister Amanda's house to spend the night. The children did not really want to go, but then, they did not really want to stay in their house either. The whole veil of doom and feelings of hopelessness that surrounded the house was suffocating and almost too much to bear.

At Amanda's house, the children all piled together on two big palettes laid out in the middle of the living room floor. They slept a little here and there but mostly they lay awake whispering amongst themselves, wondering what the morning would bring. The unanswered questions outweighed the answers by at least double. The next morning, the children got dressed in disillusioned confusion. Meanwhile, there was total pandemonium at Amanda's house, inside as well as outside. Three big, dirty dogs ran rampant throughout the house, taking time only periodically to make deposits on the already filthy floor.

At just past ten o'clock, Aunt Louise arrived. She knocked on the door but it remained unopened. Outside, Aunt called for Amanda to send the children out to her but Amanda refused. Richard was not there but he had given Amanda strict orders and now, she was not about to let them out. Amanda told Aunt Louise that Richard had promised that he would take care of the children and, if only for a short time, he felt obligated to do just that. On the other hand, Aunt Louise was not about to leave them because she had recently found out something that almost no one else knew—that Richard was a scoundrel, a rogue not to be trusted any further than you could sling an elephant by the tail. The children had become pawns in a game they did not even know they were playing.

That's how it happened that there was a mini caravan traveling to what should have been a respectful, though sorrowful, occasion. They passed the community fire department which was having a fundraiser, a barbeque sale. They then passed a car sitting off to the side of the road, still smoldering from an engine fire that had consumed it just a little while earlier. Just past that scene, Maggie noticed a light green house on the left side of the road. It was so neat and clean looking with a nicely manicured yard. It reminded her of a "fresh start." Life can be so ironic.

The cemetery was only about twelve miles away but it seemed to take hours to get there and as they rode, Maggie took in all the sights, sounds and smells along the way. That is, until her senses became overloaded, making her dizzy and nauseous at the same time.

When the small caravan carrying the families arrived at the cemetery and the children began to disembark, they were met by a parade of people, many of whom they had never seen before. Among the group of strangers were county social workers and several deputies from the Sheriffs' Department. There had been whispers between the grownups over the past couple of days that there was likely to be trouble. Maggie was not sure exactly what that meant but she knew it was possible, for her mother's family, her uncle Gerald in particular, had an oversized helping of ignorance and arrogance. Trouble. That did not even begin to describe it. What occurred could be compared with nothing less than a Mexican standoff.

On the one side were Richard, his brother, his sister and all their children. On the other side was Momma's family—her sister Louise, her mother and her brother, Gerald. Of course, Gerald came with guns, along with the attitude and lack of judgment to use them. The Hatfields and McCoys had nothing on this bunch of yahoos. The sheriff's deputies had their hands full trying to maintain peace and order. The social workers had their hands full trying to protect the children from all the idiotic and asinine behavior being displayed on all sides. In the end, both sides lost when the deputies and social workers stepped in and claimed custody of the children.

As the coffin was lowered into the freshly dug ground, a cool breeze began to blow softly, offering gentle relief to the heated environment that threatened to consume all present on this day, this turning point of a day.

Now wards of the State, possibly the children had won after all. Only time would tell.

Chapter 14
The Plan

There was no question that Momma had loved her children more than life itself. It was obvious in the way she raised them, the way she taught them about the important things of life. Love. Respect. Honor. God. She had paid the ultimate price for love; she had just sacrificed her own life by giving life to her newest son, Lucas.

Although she never mentioned it to anyone, Momma had known for years absolutely in her heart that if anything were to happen to her, there would be no telling what would become of her children. She was truly terrified at the possibility that her own children would wind up with her family. She never shared much about her childhood but what did slip out occasionally was not good. That is why back in 1962, even before Sarah was born, she had made a life-changing decision. After giving consideration to every possible outcome, she took one of Henry's homework papers and began to write on the back of it. Her simple message was to the Calhoun County Social Services. The writing on the paper was scribbled and in some places, not grammatically correct. Still, her intentions were made clear beyond any doubt. The letter read:

Excuse the paper
2-15-1962
Route 1
Clancey, SC

Dear Mrs. Vincent,

I hope this letter will not upset you or anything. Because I hope to live a very long time I guess you have had letters like this but in case of my death Wheather I am remarried or not I want my children all under 18 to be put together in an orpanage. I don't want them strung around I want them to stay together. My people love them a little I guess but I grew up in a way I wouldn't want my children to grow up I know they are having it a little hard now but with all the love they get I believe they are happy.

Very Sincerely
Rose Leonard

Now, there was no question that this informal note was not an official will. It did not refer to bank accounts or personal property but it definitely stated what Momma's wishes were with regard to her most valuable possessions—her children. Her wish was uncomplicated and straightforward. She wanted her children kept together. After all, as far as she was concerned, once she was gone, all they would really have would be each other.

Naturally, the baby, Lucas, went to live with his father, Richard. That left five orphaned children—Shelby, Henry, Maggie, Bethany and Sarah who had just turned six years old. The unique challenge of finding one place to take five children ranging from six to fifteen years old was going to take some time. It was decided that, until more permanent arrangements could be made, it would be less traumatic for the children to be placed in foster homes in the local area.

During the sixties, many foster parents were widowed women whose children were grown and gone. Mrs. Shelton was one such elderly widow woman who had been in the foster care business for decades. She loved children and was a natural nurturer. Since she already had three foster children living with her, she could only take two more. Shelby and Henry were chosen to live with her. Mrs. Nixon, also a widow, had room for one child. Mrs. Nixon preferred babies but her need for money overcame her dislike for older children and she agreed to take Maggie since it would only be temporary. Besides, Maggie could help her take care of the two little ones. Mr. and Mrs. Fielding lived on a farm and while they usually preferred to keep boys, they made an exception for Bethany and Sarah so the girls could be near the rest of the family. Even if they could not all be together, at least for now, they lived close enough to attend the same school. That way, they were able to see each other for a few minutes each day.

As Maggie lay in the strange bed that first night in the foster home, she silently said the prayer that Momma had taught them all those years ago.

Now I lay me down to sleep
I pray the Lord my soul to keep
If I should die before I wake
I pray the Lord my soul to take.

If God had taken her soul that very night, it would have been fine. At least she would be back with her momma.

PART III

A
NEW
BEGINNING

Chapter 15
New Suitcases

The winter of 1969 was a long, cold one. The Social Service people had split Maggie and her siblings up into three groups and had sent them off to live in foster homes last August when their momma had died. What else could they do? Is there a family anywhere that would have been willing and able to take in five orphans? Most likely not. That's how it was for over four months until the day finally came when they were to be reunited. They were excited to finally be back together; that much was for sure. Sure, they saw each other for a few minutes each day at school but that was not enough. After all, they had been so close before, they had done everything together. Now they were off on what looked like a new adventure. The unsettling part of this new adventure was that they would be leaving the security of their community and traveling to a distant town. They had never been more than about an hour or so from home so this expedition was like going to the far side of the earth. The thrill of getting new welfare clothes lasted only as long as it took to close the lids on their new second-hand suitcases.

It was a bright, sunny January day, but still the air was so cold, Maggie's goose bumps had goose bumps. Maggie rode with her sisters Bethany and Sarah in one car while Shelby and Henry rode together in another car. They were unsure of where they were going or what was to happen to them when they got there so they just sat like concrete garden statues for the entire journey. Only the short stop for lunch at Julia's Restaurant in Columbia broke the uncomfortable silence. The children had never eaten in a real, sit-down restaurant before. In fact, the only time they had eaten at any kind of restaurant was the couple of times they stopped at the drive-up hamburger joint in St. Matthews. The irony was that this new adventure had to be experienced under such unusual circumstances.

As they continued their journey into the unknown, each one's thoughts turned deep within, trying to reconcile the events of the past two years. Everything had been just fine until Richard had come along; then everything changed. The children did not mind sharing Momma with each other and did not mind sharing her with Richard, at first. Even so, he was still an outsider and his two boys; well that was another thing altogether. Then, of course, the baby came. As sweet as Lucas might have been, it was hard to say he was worth the price Momma had paid. Would he do something with his life special enough that the cost to Momma would ever be considered well-spent? He'd have to do something pretty significant. And if not, then the result would most definitely not have been worth what it had cost.

Chapter 16
The Joseph Marion Home

They say that when one door closes, another one opens. Now, as the vehicles drove up to the entrance of the orphanage, the Leonard children could see that the door opening was definitely different than anything they had ever seen or heard of before. The fancy arch mounted prominently over the road announced "Joseph Marion Home for Children." Immediately inside the gate on the left side of the street was the Baptist Church. Perhaps that was to remind you that God would be with you while you were here and also when you left. At times, God's whereabouts was questionable. Right now, the five had thousands of questions running rampant through their minds. With all those questions, there was no one answer that could make everything all right ever again.

The main street was lined on both sides with cottages, some newer and some older. Some were one level while others were two or three levels. For the most part, the yards were well manicured and neat. Not like rich people neat but just regular people neat—mowed and raked. Sidewalks connected all the yards and right away, Maggie and the others noticed many, many kids walking and riding bicycles up and down the sidewalks and along the roadside. The centerpiece of the campus was the elegant mansion they called Marion Mansion. A childless couple had owned the mansion along with all the surrounding land and when they passed away, they had left both land and money to establish the orphanage. Surrounding the mansion were age-old cedar trees and in the front, was an enormous water fountain filled with giant goldfish. The plush green grass made you just want to fall down and roll around on it. A beautiful, newly whitewashed picket fence surrounded the mansion and carriage house. In Maggie's mind, it created a picture that could have easily competed with any Norman Rockwell Saturday Evening Post cover.

At the Joseph Marion Home, each child was assigned a social worker, a counselor if you will, someone they could talk to about any problems they might be having. The social worker's job was to help the child adjust to this new environment while causing the least amount of turmoil. This counselor was also to help the children fit into this new lifestyle and learn to get along in a house full and neighborhood full of strangers. The social worker assigned to the Leonard children was ever so quick to point out that this was not an orphanage, even though it had originally started out that way. Rather, in recent years, it had become known as a "children's home" because many children with families, not just orphans, needed help from time to time. This notion did not make Maggie feel any better nor did it change the fact that she, her brother and three sisters were just that— orphans; no more, no less. Just the thought of the word orphan stung as much as the insult, bastard. Maggie remembered well just a month earlier when someone had called her that, a bastard. In reality, not only did she did not have a father, she also did not have a mother, at least not a live one. She felt all alone.

As the sun began to set slowly on this first day in their new world, the Leonards once again found themselves split up. You see, even though this orphanage, children's home, or whatever you might choose to call it, was equipped to take in whole families, it did not allow brothers and sisters to stay together in the same house. The cottages were not yet co-ed; therefore, Henry was assigned to a cottage at one end of the compound and Maggie and her sisters made their home in an all-girls cottage down the street.

This new arrangement was indeed a strange one for Maggie and her siblings. Before, they had shared beds, clothes, practically everything they owned. Of course, that was not really saying much for, in reality, they had very little. Now, contrary to what they had always been taught, they each had their own bed, their own clothes, their own everything. There would be no sharing, except for rooms, that is. Each room in the cottage, with its own bathroom, accommodated two girls as well as a built-in closet and built-in desk for each child. The first room down the hall was an L-shape room and was a fraction larger than the others so Maggie was to bunk with her two sisters, making three in this room. That was fine with Maggie for she and her two younger sisters were close and could offer each other comfort and reassurance as they tried to get used to this new life. The other girls in the cottage were much older, most in high school, so it worked out just fine that the younger three would stay together. As far as Maggie was concerned, the older girls could just have the rest. As Maggie looked over all her personal belongings—her blue sailor dress, her Susie Doll made of foam and wire and her doll bed—she realized that this was all that remained from the life she had had before. She sat on the edge of her bed and stared out the window. There were no bars or fences; nonetheless, the feeling of confinement was much the same. This was definitely a prison of a different sort. While they all felt isolated and withdrawn from everything they once knew, they were totally oblivious to the fact that this same prison kept them safe from who knows what.

Winter turned to spring and each dealt with things pretty much in his or her own way. Shelby would be sixteen when May 25 rolled around and she had made it clear early on that once she became of age, she would be able to leave. Looking back, Shelby had always been there for the others, especially when Momma was working. She was the one who protected them from Grandma's wrath and, at the same time, disciplined them, keeping the family in line. Now when the family needed her the most, it seemed that she was jumping ship and soon enough, it would begin to sink. But then, everyone has to deal with things their own way and this was Shelby's way. No one could fault her for that.

At night when all was quiet, Maggie let her mind wander back to the little, grey cinder block house where she had spent so many happy years with her family. After all, she was awake anyway and would be for a while yet. The new cottage parents, Mr. and Mrs. Deville, had just arrived the month before and already, they were creating a most uncomfortable environment. While it is true that Mr. Deville did not openly drink in front of the children, he did enjoy his liquor. Sometimes he could be seen sneaking out to sit in his car which was parked out behind the cottage. When he returned, sometimes hours later, he was usually red-faced and certainly not as sure-footed as when he left. He smelled like cough syrup and acted funny, always trying to smooch and rub his rough whiskers all over your face and neck. His behavior was bad enough during the daytime but the nights were even worse as he had taken up a new ritual. After the children's bedtime, he began to wander up and down the halls on the chance that there might be something to see.

Occasionally, he entered the restricted area of the girls' bedrooms under the pretense of securing the building. Actually he was hoping for the opportunity to "tuck" someone in. Though they never talked about it, Maggie and her sisters were not strangers to un-gentleman-like conduct but this place, this children's home, was supposed to be a safe haven. Because it was not, Maggie had taken up the habit of pushing the door almost closed, though it was forbidden to fully close it. She then slept with her sheet pulled tightly up around her chest. Only her toe was allowed to stick out from under the cover, and then only when needed to serve as a thermostat. Hopefully the squeak of the opening door would alert them of any uninvited guest.

Then there was Ralph. He and his brother were among the first boys to come live in the up-until-then all-girls cottage in 1971. That is when the Joseph Marion Home began incorporating their new policy of providing a "family" environment by making all cottages co-ed, boys and girls together. Ralph was several years older and when he stood, he towered over Maggie as well as most of the other girls in the cottage. It had been several weeks since the Devilles had taken the whole group, fourteen children in all, on a trip to Manteo, North Carolina to see *The Lost Colony* outdoor drama. Now Maggie tried to avoid Ralph as much as she possibly could. Though her mind tried to convince her heart that what had happened as she slept on the trip back was a dream, deep down in her heart, she knew otherwise.

Oftentimes the sadness would become overwhelming and Maggie felt as if her heart would collapse into itself. It certainly didn't help that Shelby had left the home as soon as she was able.

The family had lost its anchor and now, during these times, nothing could console Maggie and she sank lower and lower until the darkness seemed inescapable. Her world seemingly crashing about her, Maggie felt as if she was the only orphan girl to wind up in such a situation as this. Other times, after she had used up a week's worth of tears and her body refused to make any more, Maggie would sit alone, numb and unfeeling. Only after she had sanded her arm with a pencil eraser until it bled or hurt herself in some other way did the feelings return and all would be normal for a while. Of course, she wasn't the only one in the cottage to feel the need to mutilate herself. Lilly performed an almost weekly ritual of cutting herself. Maggie could understand her torment just a little bit even if Lilly's circumstances were somewhat different than her own. At least Lilly still had her mother.

The other kids, Sarah, Bethany and Henry, seemed to have moved on and begun their new lives. Things are not always as they seem, though, and how you see things depends a lot on how you look at them.

Smoking is a nasty habit. If you do not believe it, ask any of the cottage parents at the home. Sure, the Devilles were insufferable and uncaring. Still there were just some things that all adults agree on and one of these things is that children should not smoke. Even if the cottage parents themselves smoked, they still could not and would not condone or tolerate a child smoking. That is why, one evening, as Maggie walked along the sidewalk to the church for choir practice, she witnessed a most bizarre site. Jeff, from the Brickmans' Cottage had gotten caught smoking and was now paying the penalty. Mr. Brickman had sat Jeff down on a metal folding chair, right there on the sidewalk in front of the cottage. Apparently, Jeff was going to be an example for those even considering lighting up. Situated between Jeff's feet was an aluminum bucket and next to his chair was a carton of cigarettes; not just any cigarettes but unfiltered Camels. Jeff's penance for breaking the no-smoking rule was that he had to smoke cigarettes until he had smoked the desire right out of his system. He could smoke them or eat them. It did not matter. At first, it seemed pretty funny that Jeff now had permission to smoke. However, after only forty or so unfiltered cigarettes, Jeff began to turn as green as Kermit the Frog and then as pale as Miss Piggy as he began to throw up, and throw up and throw up. It was not until he had half filled the aluminum bucket that the gut-wrenching reaction to the cigarettes finally began to ease off. Maggie could not say for sure, but she imagined it would be a long, long time before Jeff wanted to see, much less smoke another cigarette.

Wakeup time at Joseph Marion was five thirty sharp each morning and all children, even the youngest, were required to do cottage chores each day. On weekdays, they were done either before or after school and on weekends, before church or play time. It did not matter what age, six to nineteen years old, there was something for everyone and always something to be done. Cottage chores included things like kitchen duty—helping to cook, setting the tables for breakfast, lunch and dinner, washing dishes and cleaning floors. Other cottage chores included things like vacuuming the big, round braided rug and dusting the furniture in the sitting parlor or sweeping, mopping, waxing and buffing the TV room or long hall. If you were young, you might have to keep the sidewalks and front porch swept. In addition to being a part of the cottage group as a whole, each child, no matter how young, was responsible for doing his or her own laundry one day each week. Together with his or her roommate, they were required to keep their bathroom and bedroom clean and tidy.

During the summer months, there were further responsibilities due to the farm being in full operation. Additional duties consisted of shucking and cutting corn as well as shelling peas and butterbeans. Bedtime, which was as early as eight-thirty for the youngest, was actually a welcome relief from the day-to-day chores that, at times, seemed never to end.

Chapter 17
Work Release

The first real taste of freedom came for most of the Joseph Marion children when they were allowed to work "outside the cottage." In fact, not just allowed, but expected. The list of available jobs was extremely long and varied. Depending on an individual's interests and abilities, he might be assigned to work on the vegetable farm, plowing, planting or even harvesting vegetables. In addition to the vegetable farm, the home operated a pig farm as well as a dairy farm. Dairy farm workers here were paid to learn how to take care of the animals and even assist with milking the cows, though the milking was mostly done by an electric milking machine. There were so many dairy cows, Jersey cows, that at one time, Joseph Marion Home was one of the top milk producers in all of South Carolina.

If an indoor type of job was more desirable, jobs were available in the sewing room. Here, while some clothing was bought and altered to fit, much of the clothing for the children was sewn from scratch. The food locker, much like a small food warehouse, also provided work for teens. While many liked jobs in the landscaping and maintenance field, the least sought after jobs were those in the sanitation and garbage collection department. Nonetheless, those too were important jobs that had to be done.

Though the usual age to begin working was thirteen years old, Maggie wanted a job so badly that she could almost taste it. She was only twelve years old but she really needed some time away from the Devilles and the constant criticism that had become the norm. She needed an outlet to help her cope with the ongoing uncertainty of her life. Perhaps time away from the cottage would give Maggie the space she needed to begin the task of discovering who she was and who she was to become.

Of course, it had not always been that way. Before the Devilles came, the Hearts had been the "house parents" and they were wonderful. They did not spoil the children rotten but they did not browbeat them at every turn either. They showed much needed compassion and all the children in the cottage, all fourteen of them, over time, began to call them Momma and Daddy Heart.

Just the thought of the Hearts made Maggie smile as she remembered the time when she, Bethany, Sarah and Peggy, the Hearts' daughter, decided to have a pajama party in Peggy's room. It was really against Joseph Marion policy to have more than one girl sleep in a bed but on that particular Friday night, they did not care. They just wanted to spend some time together and have a little fun. The two twin beds were full as could be with Peggy and Sarah in one and Maggie and Bethany in the other. Heads sticking out of the covers at both ends of the twin beds must have been quite a sight as they slept, snug as a bug in a rug.

Just because the Hearts were loving and caring, do not think for a second that they were marshmallows. They were not. Momma Heart could be firm when she needed to be. Once, Sarah, the youngest, had climbed up on the roof with one of the other kids. Sarah was only about seven at the time so it really was quite a feat for her to have shimmied up the television antenna pole which had been mounted to the side of the building. Momma Heart was aware of the situation but, concerned for their safety, waited patiently for them to come back down. Once their feet hit the ground and she was sure they were safe, she then proceeded to educate them on the proper behavior for children their age; not to mention the fact that they could have fallen and been hurt badly or maybe even killed. Yep, Momma Heart tried to keep everything at a harmonious level but sometimes it took the "board of education" to restore control.

Maggie, Bethany and Sarah spent a lot of time together. Since they were the youngest in the cottage, the others preferred not to have them around and usually ignored them. They did find a playmate in Tina, who lived in the cottage across the street. She was just a bit older but preferred to hang out with the younger kids. Tina sometimes got on their nerves and irritated them with her constant clinging and talking but, for the most part, they enjoyed each other's company. One day, Bethany, Sarah and Maggie decided to play cowboys and Indians. They had not been playing very long when Tina came over and wanted to join them. Guess who got to be the Indian? Tina. They took their jump rope and tied her to one of the big oak trees in the front yard. They played for just a short while, running around her and doing an Indian dance but soon grew bored and ran off to play dodge ball. When Tina called out that she wanted to play, they agreed to let her. They started throwing the ball at her but, of course, she was not able to dodge it since she was still tied to the tree. As it turned out, Tina was not very good at dodge ball. The three sisters, on the other hand, were given early bedtime and extra chores for their unsportsmanlike conduct.

Many things about being in a children's home were not so great but Christmas was not one of them. Christmas was a wonderful time. For the most part, the staff at Joseph Marion Home tried to brighten the children's lives, especially those who were there due to extremely sad and pitiful circumstances. Each child at the orphanage was allowed to make a wish list of three things he or she would like to have. The maximum value of twenty dollars each made it seem like the sky was the limit. Even though only one gift from the list was expected, any one of the three would be a wonderful surprise. A lot of time was spent looking through the Sears Wish Book before making final decisions for the wish list. The orphanage then sent the lists out across the state to churches and civic organizations who took on such projects. When the time came, Santa would come to the recreation center with his sack full of goodies and pass out the donated gifts to the two hundred or so children that called Joseph Marion home.

Maggie's favorite Christmas was when Mama and Daddy Heart were still there. That year, after Santa left, Daddy Heart loaded all the kids from his cottage into his truck and took them on a ride through the countryside. They rode down the winding back roads outside the orphanage gates. There was never much traffic so it was safe to travel rather slowly. The area seemed strangely wonderful, almost as if they were escaping the confinement they had been sentenced to, if only for a short while. It reminded Maggie of a movie she had seen in which the people had taken a sleigh ride through the snow as part of their Christmas celebration. When they returned an hour later, they found Momma Heart waiting with gifts for all of them. Momma and

Daddy Heart had bought presents with money out of their own pockets. It was not required nor expected but they did it anyway. Now that is love!

Maggie's mind suddenly came back to her thoughts of finding a job. Since the Hearts had left Joseph Marion, things had not been the same for sure and now she was suffocating. After searching the job list for a simple job that a twelve year-old could do and coming up empty, she decided to stop by the library. She found that by reading, she could travel to far off places, happier places, if only in her mind. Then too, she enjoyed spending time with Ms. Bellows, the librarian. Mrs. Bellows always took time with Maggie, and seemed to understand a lot of her heartache. When Maggie explained her dilemma, Mrs. Bellows offered Maggie a job right there on the spot. Naturally, because she was under the usual age of thirteen, Maggie would have to get special permission from the Devilles as well as her social worker. The Devilles were not overly thrilled with the notion but, after speaking with the social worker, everyone agreed that a job might be just the thing to help bring Maggie out of her present state of depression. Maggie promptly went to work and proved to be a good worker. She became quite proficient at her new job as library assistant and after just one year was able to run the library practically single handedly. She worked at the library for two and a half years making thirty-five cents per hour. Truth is, she would have done it for nothing.

Chapter 18
Lemons to Lemonade

Joseph Marion was not all bad once you got out of the cottage and the constant supervision of the Devilles. The hub of the campus as far as leisure activities were concerned was the recreation center, which housed a basketball court that doubled as a skating rink. Add to that an indoor trampoline, a snack bar and a library. There was foosball, bumper pool, regular billiards and television. There were ball teams to join and events going on weekly. All these things helped to create an environment aimed toward enhancing the most depressed or introverted child's self esteem; no, his life. That is, if he was allowed to participate.

Near the physical center of the campus, across the street from the recreation center, was a small park with playground equipment. There was a giant ten-seat swing set, a single set of tennis courts and an Olympic sized swimming pool, complete with two diving boards and a water slide. The swimming pool was the primary gathering place during the summer months. It was simply wonderful. Being free to swim was very liberating and good for clearing your mind and heart of everyday worries. Even so, the residents of Joseph Marion, especially the girls, were not immune to the same concerns that girls living outside its gates had. The swimsuit season brought its own set of concerns including weight, tan and puberty-related issues. In spite of these normal fears, the pool remained a favorite spot. Everyone who ventured inside the chain link fencing surrounding the pool learned to swim, either willingly or unwillingly; Mr. Brinkman made sure of that. "Sink or swim." That's what he'd say. Mr. Brinkman acted tough sometimes but everyone knew be would be the first one there if anything went wrong.

Each year, the Fourth of July celebration brought a day of good food and great fun. Everyone attended the "Marion Olympics," which started in the morning with events in running, sprints as well as distance. The longest race by far was the two-mile run. Those interested in trying that one were given a lift to the back side of the campus, past the dairy and vegetable farms and down by the pig pens. Luckily, the racing route was fairly straight and level with the finish line being at the recreation center. Running was definitely Henry's forte. He was a little bit small for his age but he could outrun a leopard if need be. He walked away with a respectable second place, losing out only to a person two years his senior. Bethany, having always been somewhat competitive with their brother as far as running goes, signed up for the race too. Not to be left out, Maggie signed up as well. Bethany proved to be an excellent runner but Maggie, obviously lacking the stamina needed to finish, came in almost last.

After a most eventful morning, a break was taken from the competitions to allow for lunch. Picnic tables, located between the recreation center and the swimming pool, were wiped down and covered with paper tablecloths, the kind that comes on a roll. A buffet of grilled hamburgers, cheeseburgers, hotdogs, watermelon and homemade peach ice cream was just the ticket to cool off the athletes and onlookers from the morning's events. After lunch, the competition continued with watermelon seed-spitting contests followed by swimming events. Seed spitting, considered to be crass and uncultured, usually had more participation by the boys than the girls but the swimming events were another story. Swimming knew no sex and could be easily mastered by male and female alike. Sarah, Bethany and Maggie were all excellent swimmers and each one participated in several events. Bethany and Sarah both scored well in the high dive and low dive competitions while Maggie took the lead in the free style and underwater races. Between them, they took home seven medals.

As exciting as the swimming and winning and eating was, perhaps the most fun part of the day was riding the tilt-a-go-round. It was a giant teeter totter merry go round that could hold about fifty people. The circular bench seat was balanced atop a twenty-foot pole so that it not only went around in a circle but it also swayed back and forth, back and forth, much like a pendulum. The merry-go round was a permanent fixture at the orphanage but on any given normal day, there would rarely be more than about six or so children on it. Holidays and other special days brought more children to ride and since the contraption was powered by gravity and weight, the more riders, the wilder the ride. If you like wild rides, that's a great thing. If you were prone to motion sickness, this was definitely not the ride for you.

Yes, each summer was full of adventure and excitement and sometimes you could almost forget your past.

No matter what else could be said, one thing had to be acknowledged about Joseph Marion and probably the other state-run homes as well. They offered opportunities that children would not have otherwise been exposed to. For example, the beach house at Holden Beach. It was owned by one of Joseph Marion's wealthy patrons but they allowed Joseph Marion to use it from time to time. That meant a week vacation at Holden Beach every summer. Just getting a trip to the beach for a week was something that Maggie and her siblings had never even thought about, much less done before coming to the home. On other occasions, the home took the children to special once-in-a-lifetime events like to hear Billy Graham speak and see Dolly Parton in concert. One of the missions of the home was to enrich the lives of its wards. The Billy Graham revival proved to be a wonderful and life-changing experience and Dolly, though just starting out, was already spectacular.

The spring of 1972 would not be forgotten; that was for certain. That summer, Maggie received her first real boyfriend-girlfriend kiss. She and Bryan had liked each other right from the start; from the first day he and his two brothers first arrived at Joseph Marion, that is. After they started "going steady," Bryan would walk Maggie to her classes and carry her books each day at school. Sometimes, in the afternoons, after homework was completed, Bryan would pick Maggie up on his two-wheeler for a ride around campus; provided of course that her chores had been completed. Since dinnertime was always five o'clock, they usually had about thirty minutes to spend before reporting back to the cottage. Many happy days were spent with him peddling and her on the handlebars.

In June, after school had let out for the summer, without warning, the news was announced that Bryan and his brothers would be returning to their family. On his last day at Joseph

Marion, a Saturday, Bryan stopped by to say his goodbyes. Not knowing precisely what to say, if anything, they just sat on the squeaky porch glider until finally the time came to leave. Bryan was shy so when his brothers called to him, he started walking down the sidewalk to the waiting car. Suddenly, Bryan turned, ran back to the porch and quickly kissed Maggie on the lips. The kiss was hurried and short; barely a peck. Nonetheless, it was still a kiss. When she turned around, Maggie saw prying eyes through the window. She slipped quietly inside and down the hall to the privacy of her room, her heart pounded wildly; her face flushed with both excitement and embarrassment. Maggie did not care. She placed her hand on her cheek, feeling its warmth. Though she was sad that Bryan was leaving, a warm feeling filled her from the inside out, as she realized that she had experienced her first real love. The memory of that feeling would carry her through much heartache.

Chapter 19
No Man's Land and Angels

The Joseph Marion Home encompassed several hundred acres. The housing compound consisted of seven residences, a recreation center, administration buildings and a modest church. On the back side of the property, there was a dairy farm, a pig farm, a produce farm and a small creek which ran to the Lynches River.

Beyond all the land that was actively used sat about fifty acres of woodland. In the center, about a quarter mile from the Lynches River, was a small, rustic cabin. Long ago, it had provided shelter for hunters. Now, aside from the small stack of firewood that had been split for campfires, the area was desolate. It was aptly dubbed "No man's land." If you had ever been there, you would fully understand the significance of the name. There were no snakes in the vicinity because the mosquitoes kept the population down pretty good. The cabin itself was a simple, four-sided structure with no plumbing, no air conditioning and no heat, only shelter. The building offered no storage facilities—no refrigerator, no freezer, no closets or cabinets, so what you had there was only what you brought with you. Throughout the year, different groups would have outings at No Man's Land. The girl scouts and boy scouts regularly set up camp to work on various merit badge projects. The remote location was especially perfect for the boy scouts' bow hunting and fishing merit badges.

No Man's Land was fun any time of year but it was the most fun at Halloween. The younger kids, those twelve years old and under, would go trick or treating around the campus. Trick or treating was normally very fulfilling for the kids as there were seven cottages, in addition to the administration buildings, and they all had plenty of candy to hand out. That added up to a lot of candy and a lot of potential tricks. The older kids, on the other hand, had the option to go on a hayride. The trip, which took them on an extended ride down winding, less traveled roads, most of which where unpaved, lasted about an hour. The final destination, No Man's Land, came into view just as darkness set in. Many of the adult staff members had a major part in the magical transformation of the plain cabin into a terrifying haunted house. The "trail of terror" was a well-choreographed walk through the cabin and the adjacent grounds in total darkness. It is amazing how much terror you can get into such a small building, no bigger than about twenty feet wide by twenty feet long. Everyone who entered did not make it through but those who did make it through, past the long-nailed fingers and never-ending screeches, the larger than life spiders and spider webs, were awarded with refreshments "on the other side." Rumor had it that even if you did not have the stomach and nerves to make it through, you still got refreshments, at least a little witches' brew or a "special recipe" candied apple. Festivities, including bobbing for apples, made the event a big hit with the teenagers. In addition, there was always the possibility of some excitement on the hayride back to civilization, especially if you were lucky enough to have a girlfriend or boyfriend.

At the northeastern corner of the orphanage property was a secluded cemetery, the family cemetery of the Marions, the couple that had started the orphanage. At the head of the gravesite of the Marion patriarch stood a white marble angel. She stood larger than life, sealed safely inside a glass case. Her hair, though nothing more than sculptured stone, seemed to flow softly down her shoulders and halfway down her back. Her eyes seemed to watch as you walked from one side to the other. Her face was gentle and kind, like that of a guardian angel. Legend had it that if you circled the angel three times, she would cry.

All of the older kids liked to go to the cemetery and do this but few spent more time there than Maggie. For some reason she thought she would be closer to God there, and she was. Often she found herself alone with God and her thoughts. "Why" was the number one question Maggie had for Him. "Why was life so unfair? Why had He taken Momma instead of Lucas? Why had Shelby left? Why had the Devilles done the things they had? Why had...?" On and on and on, the questions seemed to flow endlessly like an unleashed dam. As Maggie slowly walked around and around, she saw no tears and yet, she sensed the angel's compassion and felt that, at least here, she was not alone. Maggie sat, sometimes for hours on end, talking to God, waiting for answers to her unending stream of questions and even sometimes, getting some.

It was during one of these private talks between Maggie and God that she really began to understand some of the lessons that had been taught so many times before in Sunday school and church. She thought back on the things she remembered from Mt. Herman Church where the Marvins had taken her so long ago.

Now as she pondered them, the old things became new again. As she learned, she found it easier to try to accept the things she could not change and she decided right there to make something of her life. She would become somebody in spite of her past, not just lie down and die because of it.

Chapter 20
Make a Joyful Noise

Since arriving at Joseph Marion, Maggie had ever so slowly begun to realize that there were haves and have-nots, those who have peace and those who did not. When she discovered that those who had peace usually had God, she longed to know more. As she learned about what it meant to be saved, she began to rely less on her own strength and more on God to get her through the tough times.

Every spring, Joseph Marion held a revival and the spring of 1973 was no different. This year, however, the location was somewhat unique. The church was undergoing extensive renovations which meant that the sanctuary would be getting a complete makeover inside, from new paint to new carpet. It was going to be spectacular! In the meantime though, church services were being held at the recreation center. The revival featured preaching from local pastors as well as music by the Joseph Marion children's choir and visiting musicians. Due to the renovations, the timing of the revival was not at all perfect but then saving souls is not done on man's time but God's. In fact, it was during these most unusual of circumstances that Maggie felt the presence of God and his message in her heart. She became saved right there in the recreation center and made the decision to be baptized. When the time came for the baptismal services, the work on the church still had not been completed so the baptism took place in the community swimming pool.

Shortly after this critical point in Maggie's life, a new music and youth minister joined the staff and everyone was delighted. He and his wife were both musicians and had a true love for God as well as children. Maggie was quick to see the compassion and understanding Mr. Medlin had so when the opportunities to join the church choir and take piano lessons presented themselves, Maggie was among the first to sign up. The music and the time spent with the Medlins and their children soothed her mind and soul like nothing had in a good many years and she found that in taking the piano and singing lessons, she was able to heal some of the heartache that she had been carrying around for so long. She also discovered that through the music, she could become closer to God; a closeness that, until recently, had been absent.

As Mr. Medlin worked with her, Maggie quickly took to the piano like a fish to water. Of course, she was not great -far from it—but she did become good enough to play in church. Sometimes she played alone but most times, she played duets with Mr. or Mrs. Medlin. Sometimes they even all three played with Mrs. Medlin on the organ and Mr. Medlin and Maggie playing the piano. Over time, Maggie began to realize that her musical talent was indeed a gift from God to help her overcome the self-destructive behavior that had begun to threaten her safety and sanity. Sure, she could expect to have down times but at least now she had found a way to help her cope with them.

Even the Devilles encouraged Maggie to play the piano. Their son was some sort of piano genius so anything piano related was considered wonderful to them. First, they gave her the sheet music for "The Tennessee Waltz" to learn. It was not her favorite song but by the time she had finally mastered it, she had a greater appreciation for the melody as well as the words. Her next project, "Love Story," was much harder. Though she could never play it exactly as written, she was satisfied with the progress she was making and at the same time, was able to realize a valuable lesson. A journey of a thousand miles does indeed begin with one step. She knew that she would be able to accomplish many things, if she remembered to take it one step at a time. Patience was one thing Maggie definitely needed to work on

That is exactly what Maggie would do. With the help of her two best friends, Sue and Beth, Maggie slowly began to see life through different eyes or maybe just with a different heart. Sure, there'd still be rough patches, but she knew that she would make it.

The realization that perhaps there was a larger plan to her life gave Maggie something new to think about and after a bit, she decided that she would try to write down in words what she had discovered, or at least hoped, to be true.

When you're standing in the darkness
and you can't see where you're going
When the one thing that you need
is what you lack
The world is so confusing and
you're hanging by a string
You can't see stars until you're on your back

You'd never see a rainbow
if it wasn't for the rain
You'd never know happiness
if the sadness never came
When the road's too hard to walk alone
just take the Father's hand
And remember, it's all part of the plan

When you cannot see tomorrow
through the tears of yesterday
Just remember that
the sun will shine again
When your burdens overcome you
and you just can't seem to stand
Just hold on tight. It's all part of the plan

You'd never see a rainbow
if it wasn't for the rain
You'd never know happiness
if the sadness never came
When the road's too hard to walk alone
just take the Father's hand
And remember, it's all part of the plan

Chapter 21
Never Too Much Family

Like the other Children's Homes in South Carolina, it was Joseph Marion's policy that two weekends of each month would be considered family time. On the second weekend of each month, the children's families were allowed to visit them on campus. They could spend their time at the recreation center on Saturday or attend church services on Sunday. On the fourth weekend of each month, the children left the campus to spend the weekend with family. If a child did not have family, or could not visit their own family for whatever reason, they were considered especially pitiful. After all, who didn't have *any* family at all to love them and take care of them?

Now the Leonard children did have some real family. There was Aunt Louise, Grandma, and their uncle Gerald. Gerald was an abusive drunk so he definitely was not acceptable to the social workers in charge of the decisions regarding the well-being of the children. That was great because Gerald was not acceptable to the children either. Grandma was senile and not capable of caring for anyone, most of all, her daughter Rose's children. Aunt Louise cared about the children but she had problems of her own and simply did not have the means to take care of them. She was, however, willing and able to take Sarah and Bethany from time to time.

In order for all the children at the home to have a place to visit away from the campus, "visiting homes" were arranged, as needed, through area churches or the county social services department. These families opened their homes and their hearts to children in need and were available for the fourth weekend off-campus visits and holidays. Some even chose to visit on the second weekend of the month though it was not required. The Pollocks, Hilliards and McLeary's were among the visiting homes arranged for the Leonard children. Even though the Hearts were no longer cottage parents at the home, they still had a genuine interest in the well-being of the Joseph Marion kids, particularly the Leonard children. They initially became a visiting home for Henry; then later became a foster home for Maggie.

In addition to the visiting homes arranged by Joseph Marion, several of Momma's friends back home in Clancey, including the Grahams, the Wilsons and the Spences, expressed an interest in the children too. Of course, they could not take all of them in but then, nobody could. Luckily, all these families lived pretty close together so during times when the children visited them, they were still able to see each other.

Rather unexpectedly, in 1974, it was determined to be in the best interest "of the children" to leave Joseph Marion. It certainly was strange that, before Henry got into trouble with the social worker's son, the staff were all in total agreement that it was in the best interest "of the children" to stay together at Joseph Marion, particularly since it was their mother's specific request. Now, all of a sudden, that was no longer the case. And once again, they would all be split up. Sarah and Bethany would be sent to live with Aunt Louise; Maggie would be going to live with Aunt Jo and Henry would go to live with the Wilsons. Shelby, of course, had been gone for quite some time and was now living in Washington State with her husband.

Again, one door had closed and another had opened. One chapter of their lives was over but what would the next chapter bring?

Though it was hard to see it at the time, all four children had just been given a new lease on life. Would their new lives be better, or just different? No one knew for sure when they left Joseph Marion how things would turn out but then no one knows what tomorrow may bring. Life is indeed a mystery.

PART IV

IN SEARCH OF

Chapter 22
Memories

The orphanage had taught Maggie a great deal about life, even at times when she had not been inclined to learn. She learned how to get along with others and how to function as part of a larger group. She learned how to set a proper table and how to clean house and wash dishes. It had taught her the importance of education. It had made her realize that her music could help her deal with the emotional roller coaster called life. However, no matter what, it could not fill the void that remained; the space that should have been filled with family stuff—memories of her momma, daddy, brother and sisters, and all the other things that go along with it.

The Grahams were great but Maggie still thought a lot about her family even though they had not *really* been a family since that day in 1968 when the social service people had come and separated them. She wondered what her daddy had been like, what her momma had been like. These thoughts scared her and made her sad because over time, try as she might, the memories of them had begun to fade, especially her memories of Daddy who had died the year she turned three. Sometimes, when Maggie thought of her momma, images and questions about dying would come to her mind. "If you knew you were dying, would you be more afraid for yourself or for the ones you leave behind? Would the initial shock wear off and you just get used to the idea? What would you do if you knew the end was near? Does your life flash before your eyes, like they say in the movies?"

She thought of the times, even before Momma died, when death had tried to tear her family apart. There was the time when Sarah and Bethany got into a fight. Sarah was the baby of the family but even so, she was feisty and could easily take Bethany who was very small for her age. As the fight heated up, Bethany began to run away but, just as she turned to look back, Sarah threw a metal pipe at her, hitting her right square in the face. The jagged edge of the pipe ripped into Bethany's cheek just under her eye, causing such a bad gash, her cheek bled and bled for well over an hour. Though holding pressure on the wound did help slow the bleeding some, it still soaked a kitchen towel clean through. Bethany was terrified and even asked Grandma if she was going to die. Grandma, never one for thoughtful consolation, simply said, "No, you will not." And she did not.

On another occasion, Bethany, Henry and Momma were going to town. As Momma drove, Henry sat in the front seat next to her and Bethany sat in the back seat. Before too long, Bethany fell asleep. The Ford Fairlane was old and had developed a rusted out floorboard over the years. The hole that remained allowed carbon monoxide to seep into the car. There was neither money to buy a new car nor money to fix the hole so Henry did the only thing he could; he simply covered the hole with a piece of cardboard and, when they rode in the car, they kept the front windows rolled down, even in the winter time. All the children had been warned repeatedly never to lie down and go to sleep. On this particular day, however, the sun was shining very brightly, making Bethany squint. Eventually the urge became too much and Bethany lay down and closed her eyes. As Momma drove, she periodically checked her rearview mirror for traffic and when she saw that Bethany was no longer in view, she jerked the car immediately to the shoulder of the road. Scooping Bethany up in her arms, Momma quickly puller her from the car. After gently laying her on the grass, Momma and Henry began to splash water from the ditch on her face. All the while, Momma patted her face and whispered ever so softly, to Bethany and to God. The ditch water was dirty but at least it was wet and cool. Finally, after a few minutes of cool water and fresh air, though it must have seemed like an eternity, Bethany regained consciousness. Perhaps these events contributed to Bethany being so shy and timid. Who could say for sure?

Bethany certainly did not have the market cornered on life and death encounters. Maggie, too, had had her own brush with death. During her second year at Joseph Marion, she had come down with Scarlet Fever. Confined to the campus infirmary, she had never had so many blisters before—on her face, in her mouth, up her nose. She was on a diet of antibiotics, aspirin and ice cubes, for she could keep nothing else down. Her throat and mouth were so sore and her fever was so high for so many days that she thought she would surely die. Of course, she did not. Apparently, God had other plans for her.

Through the years, Maggie had been truly fortunate, though at times she did not realize it and probably would not have agreed if someone had told her so. Nonetheless, she *was* fortunate because she had so many people who loved and cared about her after her Momma was gone. She had the Hearts and the Grahams. Each family had opened their hearts and home to Maggie. At times Maggie was torn between them and though the resulting tension never completely went away, it was lessened tremendously after Maggie became a married woman living in her own home. Too, the Pollocks had provided a wonderful visiting home and had given selflessly to her as well, especially during the periods when their military career allowed them to remain in the area. As Maggie thought of all these people, she realized, "you can never have too much family." She had been truly blessed.

As she thought back on all the people who had impacted her life, these words came to mind:

Because of you, my life is blessed
You gave me your love and it was the best
You touched my heart so long ago
I'm saying this now in case you don't know

Oh, no matter how softly you walk
In somebody's heart, you leave a mark
My life is one that was changed
You changed it all the day that you came

Because of you happiness came
You stood there beside me in sunshine and rain
You taught me things and helped me to grow
I'll carry your love wherever I go

Oh, no matter how softly you walk
In somebody's heart, you leave a mark
My life is one that was changed
You changed it all the day that you came

Now, years later, in 1983, Maggie watched as her new daughter slept. She could not help but notice the sweet soft cheeks and the furrows that would sometimes appear on the baby's brow, making it look like a field, freshly plowed and ready for planting. Maggie watched as the baby's tiny fingers folded into themselves. With eyes tightly shut, the baby slipped the closed fist into her tiny mouth. With her blonde hair and blue eyes, she was so very different from her big brother who had dark hair and dark eyes. His skin even had a golden glow about it compared to her much fairer complexion. Maggie's mind drifted to thoughts of her own momma, as it often did since becoming a mother herself. The baby clearly had her Grandfather Walter's crystal blue eyes but Maggie wondered if she would inherit her Grandmother Rose's easy-going temperament and love of music. Though her momma had been gone for fifteen years, the sound of her singing *The Yellow Rose of Texas* could still be heard in Maggie's mind; the memory as clear as if she had just heard the song played on the radio. Life had been hard and the days long for her momma as she had tried to raise her five children on her own after her husband Walter died. Even so, Momma always had a positive outlook and a song in her heart.

Maggie pondered how her momma must have felt after each of her own children was born and how it must have been torture for her to return to the hospital just days after giving birth to the last child, Lucas. Did she know she was saying goodbye for the last time? Like marbles in a labyrinth, all these thoughts rolled back and forth through Maggie's mind. She had a wonderful husband and two of the most precious miracles God had ever sent to earth. What would her momma and daddy have thought of her family? No, what would they have thought of all of their children and their families? In total, so far, they had thirteen grandchildren and two great-grandchildren. The family was growing.

Maggie had countless questions she needed to ask. There were so many things she simply wished to share, but Momma was not there. Finally, the notion came to her that even though both her parents were gone, she could still learn about them so that her children would know about their heritage. Maggie had heard about people making family trees to record their family history so she decided to do some research and compose a family tree of her own. At least this way, her children could learn a little bit about their grandparents even though they would never have the opportunity to get to know them personally. Who knows, maybe this project would bring her own siblings closer together.

Eric, Maggie's husband, could see how important it was for Maggie to follow this dream so he encouraged her to do the genealogy research and find out as much as possible about her heritage. After all, it was not just for Maggie, but also for their children.

Trying to reconstruct a family tree was a very new undertaking and Maggie had no idea how difficult it would be. She knew nothing of the correct protocol or even where to go to find out all the information she needed. Her father had died when she was just a toddler and his family had never been in the picture as she was growing up so there was almost no information to use to get the ball rolling. One thing was certain, though. Once she made up her mind to do something, Maggie was determined. After making a few preliminary notes, she decided the first person she needed to talk to was her grandmother.

Chapter 23
Let the Games Begin

Grandma had never been easy to get along with, much less to live with. There had always been one difficulty or another in the air when she was around. It was that way even before Daddy died and it unquestionably became even more distressing afterward. Grandma had come to live with Maggie and her family in 1962 and, from the time she arrived right up until the end, Grandma had always acted as if she was a prisoner, held against her will. Everything she did, she did grudgingly and it became quite apparent in a short time that her love would not be given easily or bountifully. Maggie thought back about this fact and sighed. In her wildest imaginings, Maggie could not have known that her grandmother would turn out to be the key to so many things.

Not only was Grandma ornery, she was also more than a little senile. She had been for as long as Maggie could remember but when someone mentioned certain things that had happened in the past, her mind cleared like a freshly wiped windshield. She talked about her childhood and about her son Gerald. Sometimes she would even talk about her daughter, Louise, but not once did she ever talk about her daughter Rose, Maggie's mother. It was as if Rose had never existed, at least not to Grandma. For that matter, she did not want to talk about her son-in-law Walter, Maggie's father, either.

Maggie asked the same questions practically every time she visited and every time the lack of answers remained the same. Just when she had just about decided that Grandma really didn't have anything to add to her research, things suddenly took a different turn. On this particular day, out of the blue, Grandma unexpectedly blurted out, "She mighta got him but I had him first." That was it, the whole remark. No explanation or further commentary. Just as suddenly as she had blurted out the statement, she clammed back up. A crowbar would have been useless once Grandma made up her mind to be silent.

Even though Grandma did not open up completely about anything or give information in great detail, over the many visits Maggie had with her, she did have a few Freudian slips such as this one that lead Maggie to suspect there was much that was not being told. It would take a lot of time, and some sophisticated finessing to get to the bottom of it.

As usual, whenever Maggie got her mind set on something, she became like a bulldog after a pork chop. Her incessant questioning became a nuisance to most of her family, siblings included, but she could not help it; she was on a mission.

Because Maggie was only three when her daddy died, she really did not know a lot about him. She did not know what kind of person he was or how he took care of his family. She only knew what she had heard from the neighbors and friends of the family. That is why talking to her siblings, especially the older

two, was so important. Undoubtedly, they knew more about
these things. There was no question that Daddy loved his family
dearly for he showered them with attention and affection.
However, he also had another side, a side that was drawn to the
wild side, gambling and running liquor; at least according to the
rumors. These things did not make him a bad person; they were
just part of who he was.

Of course, when Maggie asked Henry about these things, he
did not feel ready to acknowledge this other side of his father.
Their father was Henry's hero and he would not readily sell him
short or sell him out. The fact was that even before Momma died,
Henry had been a bit distant; actually, he had been withdrawn
ever since Daddy died. He never wanted to talk about the past
and the circumstances in which their family grew up. As is the
case with anyone, indeed, his perception was his reality and that
meant he had a perfect father. Nonetheless, with a little coaxing
and a little time, Henry began to talk hesitantly about their
childhood. Though his recollection sure was different from the
information Maggie had managed to piece together, it was still a
turning point for Henry to be able discuss it at all.

As time permitted, Maggie tried to contact Shelby. With their
different work schedules and the time zone difference between
South Carolina and Washington State, that turned out to be easier
said than done. Still, once in a great while, they'd connect and try
to put together a few odd pieces to the puzzle.

Maggie talked to her brother and sisters frequently in hopes that
something in the conversation might trigger a memory or tidbit of
vital information about their past; something they might have
forgotten. Sometimes she got nothing but of course, that was not
surprising. After all, they were not especially close, even though
they were brother and sisters. It would take more time and more
coaxing. At other times, some, like Sarah and Bethany, shared

memories and feelings readily. Many of their memories were of better times, times that were full of adventure and happiness. Though happy times are usually easier to remember, sometimes they remembered things better left forgotten.

Maggie knew that each child inherited a little something of Momma's after the estate was settled even though there was practically nothing left except for a few personal items. She herself had gotten Daddy's South Carolina driver's license and a small box of black and white family photos.

Shelby, being the oldest child, inherited Daddy's merchant marine trunk. There were not really many valuables inside, but Shelby did find one legal sized envelope that looked promising. Inside, it contained two official-looking documents. One was an envelope holding adoption papers for two children and the other was a copy of Momma and Daddy's income tax return for the year 1960. Both of these items held surprises but also added to the mystery. The adoption papers, which had a Charleston County, South Carolina seal stamped on them, indicated that Daddy had adopted two children, a brother and sister in the early 1940s. Also, it appeared that, at the time, he had had been married to a lady named Hannah Jacobs.

After receiving copies of all these documents in the mail, Maggie took a day trip to the Charleston area hoping to uncover verification of the marriage and maybe even locate information on the children. She searched for two days without finding any conclusive evidence. Maggie was anxious, maybe even over-anxious. Two things were clearer than ever. This project would not be easily concluded and, without more knowledge and better knowledge, it might never be concluded. Clearly, Maggie had only a vague idea about how to go about what it was she was attempting. Perhaps she would return again in the future with a better plan after she learned how to retrieve the needed information more efficiently.

When Maggie asked Sarah about her inheritance, Sarah hesitated at first and then slowly began to move toward her bedroom closet. After opening the door wide and reaching into the dark, she produced a small parcel from the far end. In the neatly wrapped package, protected by plastic, was Momma's handbag. Perhaps by protecting the handbag, Sarah was trying to preserve all she had left of her Momma and her past.

Sarah unwrapped the pocketbook carefully. Maggie could see that it was clean but well-worn. In it, Momma had kept some of Daddy's important papers. Not important in the usual sense but rather important in a sentimental way. Included in the bundle of faded and yellowed papers were his Elks Lodge membership cards as well as several letters from someone named Bella. Neither Sarah nor Maggie had ever heard of Bella before but the tone of the letters indicated that she and Daddy had, at some point in the past, shared some very special connection. The postmarks on the letters revealed that they had been mailed from Conway, South Carolina. Maggie had remembered hearing Aunt Louise say that Daddy had lived there when he was a young man.

Also in the plastic wrapped bundle was the family bible. Maggie had not even been aware that her family had a "family" bible. The records pertaining to family births, marriages and the like were very sketchy and written poorly but together, Maggie and Sarah were able to make out some of the items. One thing they read did not make any sense. It was a notation about a child, a girl named Nora, born to Grandma. No one had ever mentioned this before. Maggie made notes about the letters and the unexplained birth and added the information to her now-expanding list of clues. It seemed to Maggie that the more questions she asked, the more questions there were to ask.

The last thing that Sarah retrieved from Momma's pocketbook was a small manila envelope much like one you would see at a bank; the kind you put coins or paper money in. The envelope contained six tiny hospital wristbands and beaded bracelets, one for each child including baby Edward. Each beaded bracelet, no larger than two inches in diameter, spelled a child's name. Now that the family's history was being pulled together, Sarah felt that perhaps the time had come for her to distribute these most precious items to her brother and sisters. They served as a reminder that their mother had loved them and had gone to great lengths to preserve the mementos of God's special gifts to her. The bracelet that belonged to baby Edward went back into the envelope and then the plastic-wrapped pocketbook.

Bethany had inherited Momma's wedding band and Henry had received a small chest of drawers. Other than these few things, there was very little evidence of the life they had all shared together in the small community of Clancey. Even so, as time passed and everyone became more intrigued with the project, they tried to share whatever stories they could remember to assist Maggie with her research. Though they did not physically participate in the search, their contributed information was absolutely imperative and now, they could do nothing but eagerly wait for progress reports.

Every morsel she learned made Maggie hunger for more. She did not even come close to being an expert; far from it; she was in fact an amateur amateur. Nevertheless, she became obsessed to the point that she could barely stand to continue with the ordinary things of everyday life. Of course, she did have to work. And she did work, but even then, her thoughts never strayed very far from the mystery that was her heritage. It became an obsession to try and crack the code of silence that surrounded her family's past. Besides working and caring for her husband and children, she found time for little else, except the family tree. Her other hobbies—cross stitch, crocheting and wood painting—would have to take a back seat, at least for now.

On her many trips to Clancey, in addition to interviewing friends and neighbors, Maggie made several scouting trips to the Calhoun County courthouse and library, both of which had extensive genealogy departments. From the courthouse records, estate records specifically, she confirmed that Momma's estate consisted of very little of value. Her children were her legacy. In fact, the estate papers showed the total value of her estate to be only eleven hundred dollars; house, land, personal property included. Maggie's heart ached for her mother. How sad for someone who had worked so hard and had given so much of herself to everyone around her, friends and family alike. It was clear that her mother's wealth was not in material things but in those things that could not be measured in dollars and cents.

Chapter 24
Conway Bound

From talking with Aunt Louise, Maggie learned that her daddy had indeed come from the Conway area of South Carolina, as indicated on the letter from Bella. Maggie decided right then that Conway would be the next logical place to investigate. Not sure exactly how to proceed and, being the amateur that she was, she placed an ad in "The Horry Independent," the Conway newspaper. Her ad indicated that she was "seeking information on relatives of Walter Christopher Leonard, born in or around Conway around January 1900." She knew it was unlikely to reveal anything useful, but for an investment of a mere seven dollars, it was worth a shot.

When she received two replies within the month, Maggie's excitement and expectations sky-rocketed. She was truly amazed at the power of the press. The first contact came by mail. Bud Leonard, from Elloree, South Carolina was researching his family tree too and had in fact, been doing so for nearly ten years already. He had come across Walter Leonard while doing research on his family line. He had kept the information in hopes that Walter would prove to be a missing link in his family tree. After sharing what information she had, they decided that there was probably no link between the two Leonard families. The little fact that they were most likely not related did not stop Bud from helping Maggie follow her lineage. He was more than willing to do research on her behalf in the counties in and around Conway since he lived in the area and was continually visiting these places anyway. During his many adventures, Bud was able to provide Maggie with things such as military draft cards and marriage records for her father as well as his father and brothers.

As exciting as this information was, more surprises were to come. Maggie learned from Bud's research that her father had been married in the early 1920s and that he and his wife Clara had had a daughter and a son. The son had died as an infant but the daughter was alive and lived just a few minutes away from Conway, in Yauhannah. It turned out that this daughter, Bella, was the mystery girl that had written to her daddy all those years ago.

Great! One mystery had been solved but the wife Clara was not the wife listed on the South Carolina adoption papers. Could Daddy have been married *twice* before Momma?

Next, Maggie received a call from a lady living in Conway. They spoke briefly on the telephone and after confirming that indeed they were cousins, they set up a date and time to meet. When Maggie arrived on the appointed day, she came face to face with Lizzie and Loretta, two of her first cousins. These were the first of her father's relatives that she had ever met. They knew immediately that they must be related because Lizzie and Loretta both looked very much like Shelby, only a lot older. In fact, they were about the same age as Bella, thirty years older than Maggie.

That wasn't really a shock since Maggie's daddy was almost that much older than her mother. The cousins said that Maggie looked a lot like her daddy. From talking with Lizzie and Loretta and looking through their family photo albums, Maggie learned that her father had had two brothers and one sister. The sister, whose name was Golda, had died as a teenager; something to do with her female parts. The oldest brother, Gene, was Lizzie and Loretta's father. Maggie would have loved to talk to him but sadly, he had died just a few months before. The younger brother, John, had died in his early twenties but his widow, also named Golda, still lived nearby.

Wow! What are the chances? They checked the phone book and after calling to verify that Golda was at home, immediately went to visit her. It turned out that Golda was not only quite elderly but also in bad health so the visit was not as enlightening as Maggie had hoped it would be. Be that as it may, simply mentioning the name of her first love, John, brought back a few moments of clarity and contentment though Golda's mind, grown fuzzy with the passage of time, was not able to hold on to them for very long.

During the course of her visit with Lizzie and Loretta, Maggie's list of questions soon turned to her father's first marriage and his daughter Bella. She hoped that perhaps they had at least heard the name. They, of course, knew immediately who Bella was but said they had not been in touch with her for quite some time. They knew that Bella's mother had died and that Bella lived not too far away with her husband Jackson. Wanting very badly to meet her newly discovered half-sister Bella, Maggie checked for a phone number and after a short conversation, headed out for Yauhannah. Bella lived right down the road from Bud whom Maggie had received correspondence previously. Since it was already past six o'clock in the evening and she still had a long drive to get back home, her visit would have to be a short one. She would return one day soon for a proper reunion with Bella and would also try to locate the cemetery where her father's baby boy had been buried in 1923. Perhaps she would even be able to spend some time with Bud and thank him properly for all of his help.

As the days turned to weeks and the weeks to months, Maggie continued her research. Whenever she stopped by to talk to Grandma and Aunt Louise, she could not help but notice how their behavior became a little stranger, a bit more strained and a lot vaguer whenever the family history was mentioned. Obviously, Maggie was getting dangerously close to the truth and getting closer to the real truth made both Aunt Louise and Grandma very uncomfortable. Who were they trying to protect? What were they hiding?

Maggie asked Grandma to verify the information she had gathered during her trip to Conway. As soon as the question left Maggie lips, Grandma instantly became defensive and when Maggie asked about the baby Nora mentioned in the family bible, Grandma closed up tight as a clamshell. Aunt Louise did too. Grandma had already blurted out the notion that she and Maggie's daddy had had some kind of relationship, but what did that mean? How was that possible? And if it was so, why didn't she just come out and talk about it? After all, it was Grandma herself who had mentioned it to begin with. Was she simply skirting the issue or trying to dodge the bullet altogether? Aunt Louise did not let anything spill either. When it became apparent that the information they were so carefully guarding was to remain a mystery, Maggie decided she'd have to take a different approach. She decided to visit her momma's cousins. She had had no contact with them since Momma's funeral. Would they remember her and if so, would they be willing to help or would they choose to follow the same code of silence?

What she discovered by visiting her momma's cousins, Irene and Belinda, absolutely blew Maggie's mind. It far exceeded anything she had ever suspected or expected to find out.

Chapter 25
The Cousins

Momma's cousins lived back in the woods; so far back that sunshine had to be pumped in for their garden to grow. In fact, if you drove west on Highway 527 to the middle of nowhere, you'd be just about half-way there. The dirt path leading to the house was usually so rutted out and overgrown with briars and underbrush that, rather than to try to drive, it was easier to park the car by the paved road and walk the mile back to the house. The twentieth century had not made its way back to this neck of the woods and, as always, Maggie had to remember to bring toilet tissue or napkins whenever she visited, as the cousins did not have indoor plumbing. They did however, have an abundance of large trees around the grounds to provide privacy if the need arose.

As always, the cousins were very glad to see any of their Cousin Rose's children though not many had visited in recent years. The cousins were simple ladies, sisters who had never been married but had chosen to live together in their family home. They had no need for modern conveniences and were perfectly content to cook on a wood stove and bath using a wash pan and water retrieved using an outdoor hand pump. As Maggie sat down, she explained why she was visiting now; that she was interested in creating a family tree and needed help with the family history. Maggie shared what information she had gathered in hopes that they could fill in the blanks or maybe even verify or dispute it. The cousins said there was much that could be told and they were more than willing to share but had decided years before never to bring it up unless someone came forward and asked to know. Now, Maggie was ready to learn, or at least she thought she was ready. This is the story the cousins told:

"Now Walter was a worldly man, a rolling stone, and, during his almost sixty years, had made his home in several towns across North and South Carolina. He was a smart man although his formal education had been cut short when his father died. As was the custom, Walter's father had left Walter his store to run. Walter had married his childhood sweetheart, Clara, as soon as she was of legal age, and they had started a family right away. Their first child, Bella, was born in 1921 and had beautiful strawberry blonde hair and a fair complexion. She had her father's physical features and was a strong and healthy child. The second child, a son, was frail like his mother, and died soon after birth, in 1923. Walter's brother, John, had died just six months earlier and now, when he was needed the most, Walter could not offer even the smallest bit of comfort to his grieving wife, for the grief he himself carried was unbearable. The house, the road around the fishing pond, the bridge that led into town, everything seemed to remind him of the plans and expectations he had envisioned for his family and his son in particular. When the grief finally became so great that he could stand it no more, Walter left his wife and daughter, without so much as a simple goodbye, to join the Merchant Marines.

Times were hard and Walter had experienced much during the Depression as a young man. Time rushed by like raging river waters during the spring thaw and in a blink, many years had passed. After wandering for a while, he found himself in a little community known as Salters. Located between Yauhannah and Charleston, Salters seemed like a good place to make a fresh start. The beaches of South Carolina called out to Walter and offered him peace and serenity at times when his life seemed to get away from him. His ancestors had all been fishermen over on the barriers islands of North Carolina and it was that same blood running through his veins that made him long to be near the coast. At the same time, even as his life began to mend, his conscience returned and before long, Walter began to feel obligated to visit his wife and daughter in Yauhannah. Occasionally, he'd make the trip and offer help when he could, although the love and happiness he once knew there had long slipped away. As he returned home time and again from these visits, Walter began to realize that he longed to settle down, to belong somewhere, to someone.

It was in Salters that Walter met Stella. As was the practice of the time, Stella kept her waist-length, black hair pulled back tightly into a neat knot on the back of her head. Her body was shapely and her skin an olive color that set off her hazel eyes. She was not a beautiful woman but somewhat handsome in a rustic sort of way. Her charm, especially around those of the opposite persuasion, could be quite irresistible. Walter was immediately smitten with her and she with him. She offered to show him around the area since he was a stranger and before long, they were spending every opportunity they could together. In just a few short weeks, they became inseparable, completely and

WISTERIA TREES AND HONEYBEES

madly in love. When Walter was around, she was at his beck and call. She was primped and primed, almost to the point of being prissy. That is how she came to be called Priss. Closer than the white on rice, better than bread and butter; the two became one. In just a few short months, Priss discovered she was pregnant with Walter's child. After waiting enough time to be perfectly sure, she shared the news with him and he did not run. Rather, he was excited to have a second chance to be the father he knew he could be.

Though they never married, Priss and Walter looked forward to the birth of their child. Priss would certainly have liked to marry Walter and perhaps she thought that by getting pregnant with his child, he would automatically "do the right thing" but he was not one to be forced against his will. He was, after all, very Irish, through and through. It did not much matter anyway because just ten days after the birth of their daughter Nora, fate stepped in and took her away. It seems that God always has a way to allow justice to prevail. Through the weeks and months that followed, Priss tried, to no avail, to help Walter heal. With no legal claim to him, Priss watched as, once again, Walter bundled up his sorrow and his few belongings, and headed further down the road.

Trying to work through his despair, Walter found a job making wicker furniture in a little town known as Lake View, near the border of North Carolina. He really loved this work and was even quite good at it but over time, he began spending his time on a more lucrative venture—bootlegging. Yes, this business was profitable and exciting, but also illegal. Eventually, the long arm of the law reached out and grabbed him and he found himself incarcerated in the Rockville Work Camp. Now this camp just happened to be within driving distance of Salters, and Priss. Although Walter tried to forget her, she kept creeping into his thoughts over and over until finally he gathered himself and went to see her on one of his weekends "off." You see, the thing about Rockville Work Camp was that, even though you were incarcerated, it was not like being in prison. The minimum-security facility offered quite a bit of leeway as far as privileges were concerned, especially for an inmate as personable and well behaved as Walter. In any event, when Walter arrived at Priss' door, he found himself face to face with not just Priss but her young son Gerald. He quickly did the math and knew right away that the boy could not possibly be his as he had been away for well over a year. Priss was reluctant to explain, but as Walter talked to the family, he quickly got the picture.

Word had it that, shortly after Walter had left, Priss had become involved with a farm hand working on the adjacent farm. The fact was that she did not love the man but she married him anyway, probably so he would take care of her. You see, that always seemed to be her plan. If she could get someone to work and take care of her so she didn't have to work, she came out the winner. If the plan required getting pregnant and having a baby, that was okay too. Of course, it did not take too long for her husband to get wise. As soon as he figured out her game, he set fire to the one-room place in the country they had shared and set out for Florida. No one ever saw hide nor hair from him again and she moved back to her family home.

As much as this news disturbed Walter, he could not force himself to stay away; he simply couldn't turn his back on Priss. There is no name for what it was, but *something* had a hold on him, something that he could not turn off. Lord knows he had tried. In an attempt to start over (for a third time), he moved to Charleston, South Carolina and married an Indian woman named Hannah Jackson. Together they had one son and adopted two more children, a brother and sister. Walter bought and ran a theatre and was successful once again, this time legitimately. He became an esteemed member of the community and had everything—a wonderful family and a successful business—or so it seemed.

Every couple of years, Walter would still get the itch and he'd have to return to Salters, to check up on Priss. Over the next four years, every time that he visited, Priss had a new beau and another child. There was Gerald, the oldest, then Rose and Louise. It very quickly became clear that Priss was the *lovin'* kind but not the *marrying* kind. No matter how many lovers she had, things failed to work out for one reason or another, so for all intents and purposes, Priss was still single. Walter continued over the next few years, to visit Priss and her children and, even though the attraction was still there, he knew he could not trust her.

Undoubtedly the result of his undying interest in Priss and her family, Walter's marriage to Hannah ended and he made a vow to himself right then to remain a bachelor. This commitment was an easy one to keep for a dozen or so years but then, as Rose began to mature into a young woman, he began to see her in a completely different light. She was quite handsome and had dark hair and hazel eyes like her mother, Priss, but, unlike the woman that her mother had become, Rose was very loving and caring.

Surprisingly, at the ripe age of forty-nine, Walter decided to settle down again, a fourth time, this time for good. Sure, Walter was more than twenty-five years older than Rose, but true love knows no age. He had been searching for so long and now it seemed that his search was finally over at long last. After the initial surprise, everyone was happy for not just Rose, but for Walter too. Everyone that is except for Stella, Walter's Priss, Rose's mother. A woman scorned? You had better believe it!

Walter and Rose Leonard married in 1950 and moved to Clancey. They worked side by side running a service station to provide for their growing family. Walter had built the station just up the hill, right there in front of the house. This made it convenient for them to keep an eye on the station as well as have their children close by. And have the children, they did. Once the children started coming in 1953, they came quickly. Between 1953 and 1960 Walter and Rose had five children. The couple loved children so much, that in January of 1962, it came as no surprise when Rose realized that she could be expecting another baby, this one to arrive sometime in the summer, possibly in July. As she ran into the house to inform Walter of this wonderful news, Rose noticed that even though he was excited, the sparkle that she had expected was not there. In fact, Walter's normally good natured-ness had been fading over the past couple of days. He admitted to being somewhat more tired lately but had passed it off as probably just due to a simple little cold. After kissing his wife and children, he lay down for the last time.

Walter had been a hard-working man who clearly adored his wife and children. Even though his health had been failing, he had continued right up until the very end to fulfill his responsibilities both as a husband and a father. He most especially made a point to do the things a father does—play with the children and provide them with everything he could. Nevertheless, because it took everything he made to support his ever-expanding family and since he had not thought or planned for the future, when it came time to make funeral arrangements for him, there was no money.

The Graham family had been in the community practically forever and Mrs. Graham's family, the Sievers, had established a family cemetery just up the road. Family cemeteries were private and ordinarily outsiders were not allowed to be buried there. It was simply not proper; however, Rose called upon their mercy and generosity again, just as she had only five years before, when her second son, Edward, had died just two weeks after being born. The Grahams were more than just casual friends and did not hesitate to assist with the funeral and burial arrangements, allowing Rose to have Walter's body buried on the property next to his infant son. Of course, the grave site was just outside the cemetery fence, just as before. This arrangement was fine with Rose and she was forever grateful for the kindness.

Walter had never held the things Stella, his Priss, did against her. On the other hand, while Stella did not hold Walter's marrying Rose against him, she certainly held it against Rose. Still, she was determined to be a part of his life, one way or the other and he was okay with that. For all the years he and Rose were married, Walter had provided for Stella. After all, she was Rose's mother, the one who was ultimately responsible for him finding his true soul mate.

That's the story of how your family got started and the secrets behind your grandma's sad, sinister, selfish self."

And with that statement, the cousins' story ended just as simply as it has begun.

The drive home from the cousins' house was a long one indeed. With her head swimming and her thoughts bouncing in a hundred different directions, Maggie contemplated what her next step should be. There was no need to confront Grandma about these new discoveries since Grandma and the truth had been strangers for quite some time. Aunt Louise, on the other hand, just might be willing to confirm the information although she had not wanted to be the one to open the whole Pandora's Box. The whole situation, when Maggie thought about it, was so far-fetched and absurd that she almost had to laugh out loud. In fact, her musical mind was already at work, putting words together.

Sitting in my lazy boy when a man came on TV
Said if you want to learn some things just come along with me
We'll climb up in your family tree. It's there before your eyes
Did some genealogy and got a big surprise

There was murder; there was mayhem and
moonshine-making men
Even found a cathouse run by Grandma and her kin
Wouldn't call her easy but she made the men go WOW
Just don't understand it. It's a mystery, even now

Oh, this genealogy is really quite the stuff
Kept on digging up dirt cause I couldn't get enough
I pilfered and I plundered just to see what I could see
Climbed up in my family tree to find out—what made me me

Fruits and nuts around me, even a loony bird
Stories going round and round, some I never heard
My dad coulda been my grandpa. Granny coulda been my ma
Momma coulda been my sister in this crazy fu-pa-pa

Oh this genealogy is getting pretty rough
Dirty now from head to toe, I finally had enough
Research went from good to bad, nothing in between
My family tree had root rot; the worst I've ever seen

Sittin' in my lazy boy, a thought occurred to me
I'm really more confused now since my genealogy
Looking through the records, still I cannot see
Can't believe it took all that, just to make me me

Once Maggie had time to really let everything sink in, it didn't really matter who said what and who did what to whom; she knew what she had to do. She had to try to get her family back together. Sure, she wanted to share the revelations that she had learned through her research and exploration but more importantly, she knew that she had to do what she could to start mending her family. Fate had separated them all those years ago but it was, hopefully, not too late to become a family once again.

Maggie had gone off in search of her past and it had indeed smacked her right in the face. The old saying, "Be careful what you wish for" came to mind. The truths she discovered had turned out to be much more than she had anticipated or bargained for but it certainly gave a greater understanding of why things happened the way they did. All these newly discovered facts definitely lifted the fog on some things, not the least of which was Grandma's attitude and actions toward her own daughter, Rose, not to mention her own grandchildren. Maggie was certain that the others, at least some of the others, would be interested to learn their grandmother's secrets. This woman, the very one who vowed "You will go straight to hell for washing clothes on Sunday," had kept secrets that would make even the most risqué talk show host blush. Yet, she projected a self-righteous image all the while to the world.

Still, how sad it must have been to love someone who loved someone else.

PART V

SECRETS REVEALED

Chapter 26
The Reunion

The summer of 1990 was almost here and Maggie had gotten the idea that it would be the perfect time to host a family reunion. It had taken Maggie over four years, between working full-time and raising her family, to complete her research; at least as much as she felt she needed to. The number of times this family had all been together since Momma's death could be counted on one hand. Now as Maggie reflected on what would be needed to pull off this reunion, she realized it would take nothing short of a miracle. Luckily, that was one thing that Maggie believed in.

Maggie had been so busy unraveling the mystery surrounding her father, mother, and grandmother's relationships that only now, as she began to plan this family reunion did Lucas, her half-brother, suddenly pop into her mind. She knew her sister Shelby had visited Lucas a few times when he was a baby but everyone had pretty much lost touch after the initial custody battle when

Lucas went to live with his father and Maggie and her brother and sisters moved to the orphanage.

Now it seemed only right that Maggie try to contact him, now that the family was going to try to make a fresh start. Maggie did not know exactly how to go about locating Lucas, but of course that did not stop her, it never did. Someone once told her, "It's not *what* you know but *who* you know." She called a friend of hers who worked with the county deputy's office part-time. She did not have a lot of information to go on, only Lucas's birth date, city of birth and the town where his father had lived when Lucas was born. Maggie lucked out though and, in just a matter of a few days, she had his address, or at least his "last known address."

Life is funny sometimes and you just never can be sure of what to expect. The best thing to do is expect the unexpected. Of course, Maggie didn't and so, upon arriving at the "last known address," they were met by none other than Lucas's aunt who announced that he had moved. Apparently, he was at a new, so far unknown, address. The aunt was more than accommodating and willing to share details about Lucas's childhood though. As it turned out, Lucas's was not an always sunny childhood but then, no one's is. What was a surprise; however, was just how twisted and troubled Lucas's young life had been. After bringing out a handful of pictures and sharing a few stories, Lucas's aunt agreed to give Maggie a call when she heard from Lucas again. True to her word, she called just a few days later with a phone number and a message that Lucas would be very interested in meeting the family.

Having no memory of his mother or her other children, Lucas was as anxious as Maggie and Bethany when they met the following Saturday. As soon as the girls saw him, they knew right away, without a doubt, that this was their mother's son. He was the spitting image of Momma but aside from the physical likeness, he was totally different. Lucas's attitude and mannerisms were so different from Bethany and Maggie's family, they seemed almost alien. Nonetheless, the three managed to have an amicable, though short, meeting.

The time spent anticipating the meeting was actually much longer than the meeting itself. After the usual small talk—"How have you been? What have you been doing?"—they were all at a complete loss for words. There wasn't really much else to say. After inviting Lucas to the upcoming reunion, Maggie and Bethany got in their car and made the three-hour drive back home, chattering non-stop the whole way. Oddly enough, although they didn't have much to say *to* Lucas, they definitely had plenty to say *about* Lucas.

During the period since the Leonard children left the orphanage, they had all grown up and moved out on their own. All were married and had families. While they had not been especially close, Maggie had tried to stay in touch with them from time to time through cards, letters and occasionally, a phone call. Maggie knew the whereabouts of most of her siblings—Shelby, Bethany and Sarah. Henry, on the other hand, had always been a different story. He had never seemed to need his siblings as much as they needed him and since he had been grown, he had become even more of a loner, like his father. Now when Maggie needed to contact him, he was missing in action. Over the last few years, Maggie had become quite the detective, especially since beginning this genealogy project. Luckily, Henry had not left South Carolina so in practically no time at all, she had tracked him down at his latest location, a small town near Little River.

The reunion was held at Maggie's home in Dillon County. When the reunion day finally arrived, she was pretty much exhausted from all the planning and coordinating but that did not stop her from rolling out the welcome mat. Surprisingly, everyone was there and that was quite a feat in itself.

Shelby had arrived by plane the evening before. She had not been back to South Carolina since she had married a soldier and moved to Washington State when she was eighteen years old. Sure enough though, she was here now, having traveled from coast to coast. The trip was very expensive; nonetheless, her husband, recently retired from the Army, accompanied Shelby on this eagerly anticipated reunion. Henry came, bringing his wife and children. Bethany came with her two boys and Sarah came with her husband and two sons. Naturally, Maggie's husband, Eric, and children Aaron and Dani were there. They would not have missed it for the world. Even Aunt Louise, Cousin Brad and Grandma came. The time had finally arrived to try to reunite the family. After all, that had been Momma's primary concern. Now, all they had to do was survive the day.

Just as Maggie had hoped, everyone began to feel right at home after just a few awkward minutes. The grownups had all settled down on the two large sofas and the love seat while the children gathered outside to play and get acquainted. Some of the children had never even heard of each other, much less met each other, but it didn't take long to get over the initial shyness. In no time at all, everyone was acting as if they'd always know each other.

Above the sounds of laughter and talking, the sound of a back-firing engine caught their attention. It was Lucas. Maggie and Bethany's previous meeting with him, while cordial, had been somewhat uncomfortable and did not leave them with a warm and fuzzy feeling. Lucas had said he would try to make it but Maggie had not really expected him to show up. Still, they opened the door and there he was.

Lucas was tall, dark and ruggedly handsome. He had black hair and hazel eyes, just like Momma's, our Momma. There was no mistaking it. Shelby had those same features too. Now Momma's family was truly complete.

They cooked out on the deck and reminisced. They had sack races and balloon shaving contests. They talked and played, laughed and cried. Although there were no doctors or lawyers among the group, they had all done okay for themselves. They had all finished high school and some had even gone to college. All had families and were working toward a fulfilling life. All, that is, except for twenty-two year-old Lucas.

Until his father's death, Lucas had lived with him. In the years since then, he had been in trouble with the law, time after time. Most recently, he had pulled time for drugs—using and dealing. Lucas made no bones about it and showed no remorse for what seemed to the rest of the group like a long string of bad decisions. As he shared all of these things, Lucas added as explanation, "I turned out this way because I didn't have a mother." Maggie's jaw dropped and her eyes rolled as she quickly turned away. She thought to herself, "No, but you *did* have a father. *We* didn't."

At first, it had been a pleasant surprise to have Lucas show up but the excitement quickly diminished as he shared this revelation. He blamed his bad life on his mother's not being there for him. Even before the meaning of his words began to fully sink in, Aunt Louise and Grandma jumped up, stormed out the door and immediately left. Maggie could totally understand their reaction. The two of them had never quite gotten over the fact that Momma had died giving birth to Lucas. They held him responsible. After all, if Momma had not given birth to him, she might not have died. Maybe it was *him* who cost her, her life, rather than her who had cost him, his life. Maggie, too, had had those same thoughts but then she realized that Lucas was the last thing Momma had done; he was part of her legacy. It is true, she might not have died. But then again, maybe she would have. Only God knew for sure what His plan was.

Before the dust from this uproar could even begin to settle, Lucas *suddenly* realized that he had to leave for another engagement. Stiff, uncomfortable goodbyes were said and he was on his way. Just as quickly as he had entered their lives, he was gone.

Now that there were only the five of them, the *real* brother and sisters, Maggie decided to share their family history as she had discovered it during her genealogy research. Sure, she had periodically given them information as she came across it; still everyone was surprised, just as she had been. It was simply overwhelming to hear the complete story all at once, unedited and uninterrupted. After the initial shock and ensuing anger at the way they had been treated by their Grandma, they all agreed that the only thing left for them to do was to feel sorry for her.

It had been over twenty years, since the family had last been together, *all* of them. Now that they had, it was a bittersweet experience. Sure, bad things happen, sometimes for no apparent reason. They happen to everyone—good, bad, rich, poor, those with family, those without family. The key is this, "Win or lose. It's up to you."

Maggie had wanted everything to be perfect but, of course, life is not perfect. She had no way of knowing then that sometimes, no matter how well you plan, things just go differently than you'd hoped; life throws you a curve ball. When that happens, sometimes you just have to pick the fly out of the soup and go on. That is life. As frustrating as it can be, you have to go on because, even when you do not realize it, God has a plan. "At least," Maggie thought, "I hope so."

By late afternoon, everyone was packing up and getting ready to leave. They had planned to drive up to Long Beach and spend the night camping so they could get to know each other better. They had never taken a trip to the beach all together. The closest they had ever come was the few times they had gone to Lake Burleigh, and then they had gone only for the day. Truth be told, the Leonards, growing up, had never traveled more than forty or so miles from home. That is until that day in 1969 when they had been picked up by the social service people and deposited at the children's home in Florence County.

At first, there was some hesitancy about spending the night at the beach and missing church services the next morning. They had grown up in different homes, with different values. They were, in actuality, strangers. Maggie tried to go to church as often as she could but she knew God would understand that this family outing, the first in many years, was important, not just to her but to all of them.

Chapter 27
Beach Bound

With two vans packed to the rim with camping gear and a
borrowed video camera, four sisters and one brother, along
with their families, set out in search of the "rest of the story," the
truths that had yet to be told. Sure, they had all learned many of
their grandmother and father's truths. Still, Maggie knew she
had some things in her heart that were aching to spill out. She
suspected, though so far she had no proof or verification, that
the others had their own secrets; secrets that could not be told
in daylight hours. Whether they would share or not was another
question, one that would soon be answered.

After a bit of arranging and rearranging of both kids and
supplies, they were on their way. The initial silence was soon
drowned out with laughter, singing and talking. The more they
talked, the more they remembered. Occasionally they passed a
landmark that reminded them of even more childhood memories.

A couple of times along the trip, they had to stop the van, get out, take a picture or re-enact some sort of childhood event which turned out looking like slapstick comedy. The group was hilarious, both the young ones as well as the older ones. Hand-held walkie-talkies kept all passengers informed of the shenanigans going on in the other vehicle.

As Shelby took her turn at the wheel, Maggie sat on the passenger side, her head resting against the window. As they rode, she listened to the sounds around her, the sounds of family. She thought, "Memories are the glue that holds a family together. When a family is broken apart, those same memories can bring it back together, mending the break." Sure, a scar, the outer evidence of a break might remain, but inside, the family is stronger.

The route to the campground took the group within a short drive of the old home place so they decided to make a little detour and swing by Clancey. Shelby, for one, had not been back in the house in years and years, not since they had placed Momma's casket there in the living room over the rotten, squeaky floor. Maggie, of course, passed the house often as she visited with the Grahams. No matter how many times she passed, she was always compelled to slow down and look, for what, she didn't know exactly. It was as if she was expecting something, or someone. They never did show up though.

On this particular day, as they turned off Highway 176 and onto the dirt driveway, the sun was fighting a losing battle. Rain clouds were moving in and looking ominous, trying to ruin the, up-until-now, nearly perfect day. The fragrant smell of wisteria filled the yard, for now it grew wild and out of control, threatening to overtake one whole side of the garage. The orange tiger lilies lined the yard just as they had a lifetime ago; only now they seemed bigger and bolder. Memories hung thick in the air like rain-saturated clouds, waiting to be released, yet daring not.

Maggie remembered how they would dig through the soot and ashes even years after the store had burned, searching for coins, glass, anything that might be of value. The chicken coop and fence were gone; now only underbrush remained. The old swimming hole, the bar pit, in reality just a wide ditch, seemed so much smaller now than it had when they "swam" and rode Henry's home-made boats in it as young'uns. The cinder block garage, with the small room over the top, looked the same, at least from the outside. The grey house, having long since worn out its pepto bismal pink coat, looked as abandoned as they had felt. Broken window glass and spray paint dotted the front porch. As they peered through the open front door, they were shocked to see that time and neglect had raised a heavy hand and taken its toll. Even though the inside of the house had obviously been updated at one point in time, the creek had risen and claimed the property once more. Now only the cinder block outer walls remained intact; a grim reminder that things not cared for soon deteriorate and fade away. Totally discouraged by the near non-existent remains of their childhood, they once again boarded the vehicles and struck out for their next destination.

Upon arriving at Long Beach, the rain, which had been falling off and on for the past hour, showed no signs of letting up. Instead, it seemed to be getting worse. Rather than camp in the pouring rain and be miserable, the group decided that they would be better off getting a hotel room. After driving around the island and finding no vacancies, at least not enough rooms for the whole group, they decided they would have to tough it out. They were going to camp after all, rain or shine. Just as they pulled up to the campsite, the rain began to magically dissipate. The sun came out and a rainbow appeared out over the water, just as if they had willed it. Maggie knew who they had to thank and she said a silent prayer of thanks on everyone's behalf.

While the grownups began the task of erecting the tents, the kids immediately found their way down to the sound-side fishing dock. The fact that no one had brought fishing gear did not weaken their desire to fish and catch crabs. Pieces of bread, moistened with just enough spit to stick them together would work nicely for bait. Bread, balled up into wads, along with a safety pin and some string could turn any kid into a fisherman. It didn't take too long before they all had the hang of it and were taking turns catching the crabs that hung out around the dock. Getting the crabs to take the bait was the easy part. Actually getting them up and over the deck railing and into the waiting bucket was the tricky part, the challenge. But then kids, especially kids in the presence of other kids, are always up to just such a challenge and can be quite creative when need be.

Between alligator-sized mosquitoes and the now intermittent rain showers, it was quite late before the tents were completely set up and ready for occupancy. When everything was finally set up, sleeping bags, picnic tables and all, it was way past time to prepare dinner. While dinner consisted of nothing more than charcoal-grilled hotdogs and potato chips, it might have been the best meal ever because the group, yes all of them, talked and laughed, even as they planned their next activity of the evening— crabbing on the beach.

Unless you have actually participated in seaside crabbing, you probably would not believe that most evenings, just after sunset, blue crabs, some small and some very large, can be found in the surf, in and just beyond the breakers. Perhaps it is the reflection of the moonlight on the water that draws the crabs out of their normally safe environment.

Some years back, Maggie and her family had discovered this and devised a seaside crabbing game. The only equipment needed were flashlights, buckets and a good dose of courage.

Once the group was divided into "spotters" and "grabbers," everyone would walk down the shoreline near the water's edge. The spotters would shine the flashlights out over the incoming waves. It was their responsibility to spot the crabs which were usually in the water just where the waves broke on the shore. Once the target was illuminated, the grabbers would try to capture the crabs, placing them in the bucket. Crabs, being the ornery creatures they are, usually required a good bit of finessing to get them completely into the bucket. Adding new crabs to the bucket, while not letting others out and not getting fingers pinched, added to the excitement of the game. The game continued until all buckets were full or everyone tired of running wildly in and out of the surf chasing crabs. In the end, all crabs were returned to the sea, usually unharmed, to live another day. This game was exhilarating and fun as everyone ran madly in circles, screaming and laughing. On this beautiful Saturday night in June, the fun lasted until about midnight.

Chapter 28
More Secrets Revealed

At just past one o'clock in the morning, with all the spouses and kids finally tuckered out and fast asleep, Shelby, Maggie, Bethany and Sarah slipped out and made their way to the campground pavilion. Henry had opted not to join them since they'd probably just wind up doing a lot of girl talking. The day had been an eventful one and, even though they were tired, they could not go to sleep. Now that they were totally alone, just the four of them, they could catch their breath and relax a bit. Bethany and Shelby handed out Dixie cups and doughnut holes. Hindsight being what it is, the combination of mixed drinks and anxiety might not have been the greatest idea given the discussion they were about to have. It did serve; however, to reduce the apprehension and get the proverbial ball rolling.

Not surprisingly, there were lots of things scrambling around through Maggie's mind; memories, questions and thoughts tripping over one another in anxious impatience. The fact was, there was no telling how long it would be before they would get to do this sort of thing again, if ever. Rather than go straight for the hard and painful issues, Maggie chose to start off easy by asking Bethany and Sarah about their lives. They were the youngest and would most likely be the easiest to get to talk.

Bethany and Sarah were ready to share their experiences, at least *some* of their experiences. They told about their lives with Aunt Louise and her husband, Bert. Aunt's single-wide trailer only had two bedrooms and, with their son Brad, there was really no room for more children. In spite of this, the orphanage had still sent Sarah and Bethany to live there, along with the promise of a monthly check. At first, Bethany and Sarah slept on the pullout couch in the living room but eventually Bert built on a room for them. Actually, it was more of a shed since it had not been built to code and had no heat or air conditioning. In the summer time, the tin roof helped to heat up the room almost to the point of being stifling. The winter was almost as bad because, with no insulation, the room was freezing, almost. At least in the winter they could warm their bed by running the hair blow dryer between the sheets for a while, and they did have that old wool army blanket, even if it was itchy. Still, they had a space they could call their own, sort of. Then there was the dog situation. Both Bethany and Sarah were always animal lovers but living with three dogs, and big dogs at that, made sanitation a real problem. The dogs made messes inside and out, usually resulting in Sarah and Bethany having to clean them up, if the messes were to be cleaned up at all.

Maggie was the next to speak. As everyone sat in total silence, she began her story. "Shelby, remember when I went to visit you when you lived in Columbia just after you got married? You found a book of hand-written poems in my bag. You even read one of them. Well, the one you read was about the night Momma went back into the hospital after Lucas was born. We were all at Richard's house waiting to hear that we could go to the hospital to see her. Finally, it got late and we all went to bed, the boys in one room and the girls in another. I thought everyone was asleep so I just lay there quietly, listening to the sounds of everyone breathing. Sometime later, Richard came home from the hospital and quietly slipped into the bedroom where you, I and the other girls were sleeping. You and I were together in one bed with you on the side closest to the door. When he came in, he knelt down by you and whispered, asking you to come into his room with him. He said he had room in his bed and you would not have to be crowded. Of course you did not go. It was at that moment that I realized something that I had not seen or been able to grasp over the past two years. This man, whom our Momma had loved and trusted with her children and her life, was a rat. The fact the he was a rat certainly helped to explain the way his two sons acted. Children learn what they live; that was why they were just like him. Of course, that did not justify it but it did help explain it."

Shelby sat stunned; tears filled her eyes and slowly began to trickle down her cheeks to the corners of her mouth. She had had no idea that anyone else knew about that night, about Richard. There was really nothing that she could say, nothing that she needed to say. Perhaps the fact that this secret was now out in the open could offer Shelby the tiniest bit of comfort knowing that she did not have to keep it to herself any longer. She could finally let it go.

Maggie continued.

"When Momma and Richard were dating, they left us at Richard's house with the older kids watching out for us. Remember? Well, didn't you ever wonder what went on sometimes after Bethany, Sarah and I went to bed? You all would be partying, you know, listening to *Hello Mary Lou* and *Lipstick on Your Collar* and dancing around, having a good time. Richard's oldest son would come back into the bedroom and ask if I wanted to join the party. Of course, I wanted to be with you and the older kids but instead of going to the living room where you all were, he took me to the other bedroom and made me lie on the bed. He pulled my pajamas down and, after he got his jollies fondling an eight year-old, he returned to the party. Apparently, no one ever suspected; at least no one that could do anything about it.

At nine years old, Jimmy was just as bad even if he *was* the younger one of Richard's sons. He tried several times to get Bethany and Sarah to take off their clothes. I remember finding him with them in the horse stable one time. He told them, 'Do it and I'll let you ride my horse. Take your clothes off and I'll take off mine.'"

As Maggie spoke of these unspeakable things, Sarah and Bethany sat with their heads down, nodding silently but not speaking. Then Bethany looked up, tears in her eyes. She talked a little saying, "That wasn't the only time something like that happened." For her whole life, Bethany had been bashful and so without giving too much detail, she began to tell about a time, before the orphanage, back at the foster home. The other two foster children, two boys, were much older than she was. One day, while doing her chores, one of the boys cornered her in the barn. She was so small, she could not fight him off and later, after it was all over, she was too scared to tell anyone. She never did either, until now.

Sarah, who had lived with Bethany for most of their lives, was both shocked by the incident and saddened that she had not known about it. She, herself, had never experienced this type of thing but it certainly was not for Aunt Louise's husband Bert's lack of trying. He never drank during the week but when Friday evening came, he felt he had earned the right to drink and he most definitely exercised that right. He also thought that, by providing a place for Sarah to sleep, he was owed whatever he wanted from her. If it had not been for Aunt Louise, there is no telling what might have happened. Eventually, Sarah was old enough to get a job and move out. If she didn't have to be there, she didn't go there. As she gained more self confidence, when she did have to be there, she was able to put the brakes on Bert whenever he threatened to get out of line.

Maggie continued. "Do you guys remember playing hide and seek when we were little? Remember the time when we were playing and Henry went missing?" He had been missing for what seemed a long time so we all stopped playing and began to seriously look for him. We looked behind the house and under the house, in the chicken coop, even in the tree house. We looked in the horse barn and in the old black, broken down Buick. When we went to look by the garage, we could hear Gerald's voice. At first we couldn't make out what he was saying so we decided to scrunch down behind his car so we could jump out and scare them when they walked by. As we waited in silence, Gerald's voice became clearer and uncharacteristically gentle. Just then we heard him say, 'I'll give you a nickel if you promise not to tell anyone. It'll just be our little secret.' Did I imagine that or did the sick bastard molest Henry?"

Bethany and Sarah were too young to remember but Maggie could tell by the look on Shelby's face that she remembered and knew the truth.

Silence filled the now-empty air as they all sat, staring, not really at each other; but rather *into* each other. Just then, they heard the crunch of gravel as Henry appeared from behind a tree next to the pavilion. They did not know how long he had been there, but from the look on his face, they knew he'd been there long enough.

Henry came in without a word and sat quietly in the corner, acknowledging nothing. His thoughts were his own as Maggie continued.

"Remember when I was sent to Mrs. Tyler's to stay? Richard's two nephews, Michael and Robert, would stop by and visit every week or so. They liked to do the visiting outside so Mrs. Tyler would not be within earshot range. Now, looking back, that may not have been the wisest choice. The visits seemed nice at first because it appeared that I had not been forgotten, after all. Nice, that is, until one Sunday evening, we were standing out by their car. Bob said he had to take a pee and walked around the back of the car. Michael asked if I would like to sit on the hood of the car and then he helped me up, sliding me up his body as he went. He started smiling, talking all the while, telling me how pretty I was and after a few minutes, he kissed me, first on the cheek and then on the lips. Well, no one had ever kissed me before. It felt nice and gave me a warm, loved feeling. Before I knew it, he kissed me again, this time sticking his tongue in my mouth and putting his hands, first on my legs and then sliding them upward. In shock, I jumped down and ran in the house. At the time, I didn't really know much about this sort of stuff but I did know that it didn't seem right."

Maggie then related how alone she had felt at Mrs. Tyler's. Originally, Maggie went to the same foster home with Shelby and Henry but then was moved to Mrs. Tyler's. Try as she might, Maggie could not hide her disappointment at having been taken away from Shelby and Henry. In any case, Maggie's loneliness must have been apparent to Mrs. Miller, her fourth grade teacher. That is why every day after lunch Maggie went to her saying she did not feel well. Mrs. Miller would excuse her from school, allowing her to walk home alone to Mrs. Tyler's house, which was right up the street. Even though she probably knew that Maggie did not go home right away, Mrs. Miller let her go anyway. Rather than go home, Maggie stopped every day at the big oak tree next to the Baptist Church, which stood between the school and Mrs. Tyler's. There she sat, day after day, leaning up against that tree, where she stayed until she was expected home from school.

After Maggie had finished this tale, she stated, "But now I have a question for you, Shelby."

She had been thinking about this for a long, long time but knew she'd have to approach the subject carefully.

"During the time that I was staying at Mrs. Tyler's, I went to spend some weekends with Uncle Rob and Aunt Jo. One weekend, I remember Aunt Jo taking me to visit you in the hospital at St. Matthews. There has been a question lingering in my mind for the longest time and I have never had the opportunity to ask it before. What was that all about?"

As one might imagine, Maggie surprised Shelby with the question. Shelby had not remembered receiving any visitors during her hospital stay. But then, she probably did not remember much of anything about that hospital stay; it had happened so long ago. Now all these years later, she knew.

Shelby took a long, slow breath and began to explain, "The weeks and even months after Momma died did not seem real to me. It was more like a dream; a bad, bad dream. At least that is what I had hoped and made myself believe. I kept telling myself that I would wake up and Momma would come and get me from the foster home. Not that Mrs. Shelton was bad. She was not. I loved Mrs. Shelton. She was a wonderful and loving foster mother but she was not Momma."

Certainly, that was true.

"I do not really remember exactly what happened during that period of time but what I was told was that one day Mrs. Shelton came out to find me sitting on the front porch swing, rocking back and forth, with my clothes in a brown paper bag next to me. When she asked me what I was doing, I told her I was waiting for Momma to pick me up. She sat down next to me and hugged me, and told me that Momma was gone and would not be coming for me. That is when I lost it. They said I had suffered a break with reality. After many, many sessions with a counselor and many days in the hospital, I finally came to realize that my mother truly was dead and that she would not be coming back for me. They said the break was due to the death of my mother but also the death of my protector."

"You see, long before the incident with Richard, we all had to deal with the constant threat of Gerald. Sure, he was Momma's brother, but he was absolutely the worst person we had ever known, possibly the worst we ever *would* know. Gerald was nothing short of a total sadistic drunk. He beat his wives, all three of them. Some even thought that that was why his son was born the way he was. He beat his sisters and he beat us, at least those he could get his hands on, away from Momma's watchful eye. At other times, though, he seemed completely different. During those times, he was still a drunk but he was not hateful like before; he was worse. It seemed like every time he showed up as this alter-ego, he had been drinking whiskey instead of the usual beer. And not just one drink either, he would usually down the whole bottle at one sitting. He would start to act silly and try to smooch all over us. 'Come, give Uncle Gerry a kiss,' he'd say. Grandma thought it was so cute, but then she thought the sun rose and set in her delinquent son."

"One day when I was about twelve, while Momma was at work, Gerald showed up. I was helping Grandma to fold the laundry. After we had finished the laundry, Grandma sent me out to the garage apartment to get something. Gerald had gone to the apartment and was sleeping off the night before. Once I realized that he was there, I became especially mindful of the noise I was making and instead, tried to move unnoticed to the far end of the room. Now that the apartment was not occupied, it was full of clutter and the walkway between the piles of boxes and things was narrow with barely enough room to walk through sideways. Just as I tried to inch my way quietly by the couch, my foot touched a piece of paper, making a crumpling sound as I quickly picked my foot up. I thought I had made it when suddenly, without raising up off the couch, he stretched out his arm and grabbed me around the calf.

Gerald looked relatively scrawny compared to when he was in the Army but he was much stronger than he looked or at least much stronger than I was. At first, he started saying, 'Oh come on Shel, sit on Uncle Gerry's lap and give him some sugar. Can you feel how much Uncle Gerry loves you?' He acted all lovey, dovey, but as soon as he dragged me down onto his lap, I knew I was in trouble. Before I could jerk loose and scramble out the door to safety, he grabbed me by my arms, forced me down to the couch, pulled my dress up, and did his business. After what seemed like forever, he passed out again and I was able to run back in the house. Crying, I tried to tell Grandma what had happened but she would have none of it. Her immediate reaction was to slap me across the face and yell at me, telling me not to tell lies about Gerald.

"He would never do such a thing as that," she said. "He could have any woman he wanted, he certainly don't have to resort to messing with kids." She warned me that I would be in a world of trouble if I ever told anyone, above all Momma. You know Grandma; she was a bitch and, probably the original one."

What a revelation! Everyone knew that Gerald was a scumbag, but this was totally beyond anything they could have imagined. His own niece! The feelings of sympathy that Maggie had begun to feel for her grandmother over the last few months vanished in a flash. How could she have ever felt sorry for her? Now she despised her grandmother more than ever.

Henry had, for the most part, been sitting quietly, apart from the others. After saying something in a super quiet voice and getting no response, he grew louder. Once everyone became silent and gave him their full attention he repeated, in a timid voice, "I killed Daddy. It was all my fault."

When Sarah asked what he meant, Henry explained.

"In January of that year, I came home from school one day with my ear hurting pretty bad. I had had a stuffed up head and a sore throat for a few days and evidently, it had turned into an ear infection. The winter had been a tough one for Daddy too. Even though he kept going to work, each day he seemed to be a little more tired when he came home. That day, Daddy came home a bit earlier than he usually did and when Momma told him I had an earache, he immediately told her to take me straight to the doctor. We really did not go to the doctor very often; you all know that but, for some reason, he sent us. I guess he could tell I was in real bad pain with my ear. He said he would stay at the house and look after the other children.

When we returned from the doctor's office, Daddy was sitting on the couch with his head laid back, looking very pale. The doctor said that I had an ear infection but a round of antibiotics would have me as good as new in a few days. When Momma asked Daddy how he felt, he told her that he was not feeling all that great. In fact, he said he was just here and nothing extra and that he would like to lie down on the bed for a while before supper. With that, he got up, kissed Momma on the forehead, went into the bedroom, pushed the door to, lay down on the bed and died. If only Momma had taken Daddy to the doctor instead of me, then Daddy would not have died."

Everyone scooted over to where Henry, now crying uncontrollably, sat. In all the years, none of the girls had seen Henry cry, much less bawl like this. Now, at last, he was letting go of years and years of guilt and probably hurt and anger too.

All huddled together, the tears flowed freely between the five until all their faces were quite pale and salty. The only color that remained was the black from the mascara that once adorned the girls' eye lashes. Once their composure had somewhat returned, they all tried to assure Henry that Daddy's dying was not his fault. If Daddy had been ill, and apparently he had been, then he should have told someone. How could any of them, being children, have known or guessed what was happening? How could anyone have known how serious his illness was?

Henry had nothing further to say about this or anything else.

When the group returned to their campsite, they discovered that the sleeping arrangements had been revisited and that only one tent remained unused; the large tent that would be big enough for all five of them.

As calmness once again began to settle, the five scooted down into their sleeping bags, side by side. They were completely exhausted, both physically and emotionally. With each experience shared, the sick feelings inside each of them had intensified to the point of nausea and then, ever so slowing, had begun to diminish as they shared the burdens they had each born alone for so many years. Their heads were literally swimming. This might have been in part due to the large amount of rum and vodka they had consumed. Mostly, though, it was from the things that had just passed through their ears and into their minds and hearts.

Maggie had had no idea, when she started this confession session, what would happen. Many of the experiences they shared were similar and yet each one unique. The experiences had left the siblings with feelings of sadness and guilt. Though things had been out of their control, they still felt responsible and accountable. For the past twenty-odd years each had felt almost like an only child; an only child that had experienced the injustices of a cold, cruel, uncaring world. Now, hearing the others acknowledge things that had been hidden up until now, they each realized that, in fact, they had not been alone. Quite the contrary, they had actually been connected in a way that they could not have imagined. They could feel empathy as well as sympathy for the others and, at the same time, take comfort in knowing that someone else shared and understood their feelings. They had each, in their own way, dealt with things over the past years. Now it was time to let go of the hurt, the hate, the guilt and the pain.

All of these things, all of the events of their lives had directly or indirectly been the result of Grandma and the selfish choices she had made. She would have to answer for that, but not to them. She would have to answer to a much higher power.

As alone as each one had felt more than once over the last two decades, they all acknowledged the relief they felt now, realizing that they had survived. They each had spent so many years as an only child when the bond was there all along. All they had to do was cement it and tonight they did just that. A single twig is not very strong but a bundle of twigs is. That's why right there in that tent, in the middle of a rain-soaked campground, the five made a vow. They each vowed to be there for the others in the future, no matter what the future might bring. It might not always be convenient or fun, but now that they were a family again, they had a responsibility, not just to themselves but also to each other.

After each had emptied their hearts, and some, their stomachs, they slept.

Chapter 29
Closure at Last

As the rain began to ease up a bit, Maggie let her mind wander back to that trip, to the emotional roller coaster and exorcism that she had not only witnessed but also participated in. She pondered a question that had been asked so many times, in many different ways. "Do people fail because of their past or do they succeed in spite of their past?" From what she could determine from spending time with her family, most of them had flourished in spite of their past. Then again, was it *because* of their past? Lucas, on the other hand, had lived a very different life. He seemed to have chosen a completely different path. He used the loss of his mother as an excuse to go astray rather than use it to become a stronger, better person. He even acted as if the world owed him something.

Grandma had lived to be ninety years old and, in all those years, Maggie could not remember the last time, if ever, she had smiled or even made someone else smile. Her bitterness at having lost the love of her life had consumed her to the point that bitterness was all she had left to give. Walter, Maggie's father, had wanted her enough to return repeatedly, only to find she had been "looking for love in all the wrong places," as the song says. When she finally decided that he was the one that she wanted to settle down with, it was too late. Fate had stepped in and Walter had fallen for none other than Rose, her own daughter. Sure, life had thrown Grandma a curve or two, or had it been her throwing the curves? In any event, the irony is that while she pined away for a man who no longer needed or wanted her, she closed her heart not just to her own family but to any possibility of finding happiness with another man.

Now as they lowered Maggie's grandmother's body into the cold, dark ground, Maggie was sad; not so much for the loss of her grandmother, for she had never really had a grandmother, at least not in the traditional sense of the word. That is what was saddest of all. At least now, though, Maggie was sure she and the others could get on with their lives. They had finally been able to make some sense of the perplexity that was their lives. For now, they could understand, if not forgive, their grandmother's actions. Maybe someday they would even be able to forgive her. In the end, Grandma had hurt herself more than anyone else. She had missed out on all the blessings that five wonderful grandchildren would have brought to her life.

Once back inside her car, Maggie turned the radio off so she could drive home in silence. She passed by unfamiliar sights and familiar sights; all the while her mind wandered. *No matter how*

185

softly you walk, you always leave footprints in the minds of those who knew you. Maggie had heard that, or something like it, years ago and it had stuck with her. Now, more than ever, she realized the saying was absolutely, unequivocally true. Richard and his sons, Maggie's grandmother, her aunt and uncle, the foster homes and visiting homes. All these had been a part of Maggie's life, some for shorter periods and others for longer periods. They all had a life-altering effect. Momma had been given only thirty-six short years on earth but during those few years, she had made a positive impact that would last a lifetime. Maggie knew that, like her mother, she would always strive to see the beauty in life even when it was not always sunny outside. It would be a challenge but she would see it through.

Yes, the journey had been a long one, filled with twists and turns, ups and downs. As Maggie quietly reflected on all these things, she thought of her next project. Some of her adventures and experiences, though sad, were ultimately enlightening and helped to make her stronger. Perhaps she would use some of the things she had learned and maybe compose a song or two. Lord knows, her music had certainly carried her through most of it anyway. Then too, as of late, she had taken up humming, like her mother, and on occasion, even sang a bit. She was not very good at it but, with a lot of practice and a lot of prayers, she could be.

The thought of singing made Maggie smile and she decided to switch the radio back on just as the old bluegrass song, "Genealogy" began to play. She thought about the next family reunion and a smile came to her face. Who knew what new truths might be uncovered between now and then? Maybe the next time her family got together, it would be at the old family home place in Clancey. She could see it now—bright red and blue blankets spread on the lush grass, picnic baskets opened with food spilling out. Everyone would be sitting, casually leaning against each other, picking back and forth, and laughing. Yes, laughing.

They would sit and reminisce, breathing in God's fragrance, amid the wisteria trees and honeybees.

About the Author

Born in North Carolina, Donna was the sixth of eight children. She learned early on what it was to be a family. Though she had been writing poetry since she was eleven years old, Donna did not submit for publication until 1988 when her poem *AnNe* was published. Since then, she has had others published including *Ten-Year Thank You, A Higher Vision* and *The Tribute*.

After the September 11, 2001 terrorist attacks, Donna felt compelled to pursue her artistic side further, both by writing poems and by writing music for some of them. Her first published song, "As Americans We Stand," was included on the Songwriter Album American Pride, released by JIP Records, of Nashville, Tennessee in 2004.

Donna's creativity through literature and music is her therapy but she also hopes it is an inspiration to others.

Donna resides in central North Carolina with her husband. They have been married for thirty years; have two children and three grandchildren.

What others are saying:

"The story is mind-boggling in its authenticity and it keeps you wondering what can happen next to these dear children. Many may not understand that this is life in the raw. It is what life is really all about to many people, some we may know and some we may not. It is amazing that they came through the fire of affliction so well, in spite of the fact that life was so mean and unkind to them for so long. Their experience proves that faith is a strong defense against the horrors that life can send your way. This family proved that fact without a doubt. Good writing and good reading. What more can you ask for? If you knew Donna personally as I do, you would see what an amazing person she is and would know how she came up with such an interesting and arresting book."

—Rosemary Gain, Author, *Mom-Mom's Rocker*
Website: http://potpourrioffaith.com/index.htm

"Outstanding. I didn't want to put the book down. I found that Maggie and her siblings found a genuine love from their momma, Rose. After she died, all of their lives were turned upside down because of her absence. Some were able to come out at the end with God's help. He was there all the time, only some saw his works."

—Mary Ann Parrish

I have just finished reading "Wisteria Trees & Honeybees" (wonderful title). I think it would make you want to know what was inside. I found the book to be very good reading and a story that is very believable. It kept my attention throughout the entire time. I do read a lot of books by Lori Wick, Peggy Stokes, Nicholas Sparks, Karen Kingsby and others and I would say that this book was equally as interesting.

—Barbara West

Manufactured By: RR Donnelley
Breinigsville, PA USA
April 2010